SANJAK . . . son of the wind and rain and open prairie, a leader of the Kiowas . . . magnetized by the quiet spirit and inner strength of his Mexican Woman, taken in a raid. What was the source of her beauty? For what purpose had she come into his life?

ILEETA . . . stolen, terrified, from her village in the middle of the night, her baby torn away and left to die along the trail northward . . . plunged into an alien household at once strange and yet curious about her "medicine," as they called it, the man on the cross that hung from her neck.

THE WHITE MEN . . . traders, soldiers, buffalo hunters . . . relentlessly pushing for more land, more control, determined to civilize these savages into a manageable minority, if not by persuasion, then by force. . . .

With divergent characters such as these Elgin Groseclose has woven a powerful tragedy of two races on a collision course. In the midst of the turbulent 1860s, Sanjak searches for the meaning of the faith most white men espouse but few seem to practice . . . and none as completely as his beloved Ileeta.

D1477509

ELGIN GROSECLOSE

David C. Cook Publishing Co.
ELGIN, ILLINOIS—WESTON, ONTARIO

F

11-28

Edited by Dean Merrill
Designed by Kurt Dietsch
Cover illustration by Lois Hatcher
Printed in the United States of America

ISBN 0-89191-113-8 (paperback)
LC 78-55386

ISBN 0-89191-114-6 (hardcover)
LC 78-55386

To
my dear sister
Esther Damm
for her urging
that our native region held
a story to be told

Author's Note

This is a work of fiction, and should be read as such, but is based upon characters and incidents of the Southwest during the period preceding and following the Civil War.

PART

I

The
Medicine

ONE

It was from the Woman taken in the raid on Santa Rosa that Sanjak obtained the amulet he called his Medicine. The Woman, whom he named Ileeta, he had obtained from Running Wolf.

The Woman had gone to Running Wolf as his plunder, but by one view she should have belonged to Sanjak from the first. Running Wolf would not have come out alive, with the Woman across his shoulders, but for Sanjak's timely aid.

They had gone down to Mexico for horses and women—twenty-six braves, of whom twenty were Comanches and six were Kiowas. In those days the Kiowas were like younger brothers to the Comanches, a smaller people but equally warlike. This happened before the time the white men went to war among themselves, when between the Red River and the Rio Grande settlers were wary and the Texas ranchers vigilant. Mexico was easier territory for the braves, and there were many poorly protected villages and haciendas.

They were under the leadership of Yellow Horse, a redoubtable warrior of the Kiowa Red Leg Society, of which Sanjak was a member.

Avoiding Fort Duncan on the Rio Grande and keeping to the west in the mesquite and chaparral country, Yellow Horse had brought his party to a village not far into Mexico. The village had a horse market where buyers for the Mexican army came to obtain mounts.

At a distance from the village, behind a thicket of organ cactus, the raiding party dismounted, and Yellow Horse told three of the younger braves to watch the horses while the others went on the raid. Sanjak was not one of the younger braves left with the horses. This was not his first raid. Only Yellow Horse with two or three of the Comanches, and Running Wolf of the Kiowas, were more experienced in battle.

Everything was still, except for an occasional cry of an owl and the neigh of a restless pony. The moon was high, and they waited until it had set. It was toward morning before they attacked.

It was a methodical business at first. Like their periodic buffalo hunts to restock the jerky lines, these were to acquire ponies for the herd, and women for the tepees, and possibly silver and trinkets for the squaws. But however deliberately the plans were laid, however severe the discipline imposed by the leader, as they approached the quarry, the zest for battle rose like a fever infecting the band, beginning with the youngest.

Sanjak was acquainted with the symptoms—the tightening of the tendons, the activity of the kidneys, the quickening of the heartbeat, the constriction of the lungs, the sudden blurring of the eyesight. At the moment of assault, however, all these would pass, would dissolve in a blood lust and fury of passion; then the eye regained its vision, the arm its strength, the mind its wariness. It was the return of these faculties of control and decision that had brought him unscathed through so many similar situations.

On this occasion, however, the scent of battle was missing. For some reason strange to him, his medicine—mysterious substances from the tribal medicine man that hung in a little sack from his neck—did not reassure him. He sensed something amiss. Crouching along a ridge above the village while he waited for Yellow Horse's signal, he shifted on his knees, then rose and peered through the bushes at the village below. He wanted to detect, if possible, what might be wrong, to see some evidence of premature discovery, some unexpected resistance.

The houses were of adobe, unplastered, Sanjak noted, as they are where the people are not rich. It did not seem a likely object of raid, except for the horses. The streets were narrow, which did not make fight or flight easy. From one of the courtyards a wisp of smoke arose, no doubt from some outdoor caldron—the Mexicans, it seemed, were forever washing their clothes—and the adobe walls in the moonlight resembled the underbelly of a canyon deer.

The thought of the likeness stirred in Sanjak a memory of an earlier incident—one that happened when he was much younger, before his first venture on a warpath, when he was hunting with a couple of older companions.

He had crept toward a clump of tamarisk in which he scented game. There was a movement among the branches, and he had shot an arrow into the clump. No sound followed, and Sanjak had rushed forward to seize his prey.

It was a fawn, and as it lay prone, its legs quivering, Sanjak raised his hatchet to finish it off. The fawn had turned its head as Sanjak broke in, and its large eyes were fixed on the hunter with that quality that no man understands but reads either as terror or trust. In that moment, something passed between the beast and the Indian and filled Sanjak with an uncertainty of purpose that long afterward continued to puzzle and trouble him. He turned away, unable to strike. A little later, when the fawn was dead, he severed the head, removed the arrow, skinned and dressed the carcass, and brought it back to the lodge.

"You should not have killed it," his mother, the squaw Sweet Grass, had scolded. "Especially as it was a doe."

"You talk too much," Sanjak had replied, but he remained troubled, for he was very young then. Many times thereafter he would go out in the night to listen to the frogs crying and wait for a star to fall, meditating on the mystery of life and death, until Sweet Grass, who had an intuitive understanding of the deep things in Sanjak's nature, would counsel,

"Sanjak, you see much in the heart. When you grow up, you will become a powerful medicine man. You will see the Great Spirit, and you will utter what the Great Spirit may say to you."

But Sanjak did not become a medicine man. Adventure drew him, and danger was a challenge. He was skilled in the making of bows and arrows, and in their use, and later, in the use of the white man's long rifle. He was invited to go on raids; and by age twenty he had been on two major raids—one of these on a wagon train in which he had been wounded and captured. He had spent a summer in a stockade before he had managed to escape. During that time he had learned a smattering of the white man's language. For this exploit, his escape, and especially his new ability in speech, he was initiated into the exclusive Red Leg Society of warriors. Besides his acknowledged skill in war, Sanjak was shrewd in trade, and though not given to much speech, respected for his counsel. He was now, at twenty-three, the owner of fifty ponies, the wearer of three scalps on his belt, and the husband of two squaws. . . .

A fringe of cloud appeared in the west, into which the moon dropped; the sky grew dark. It was near dawn, and Yellow Horse sent Sanjak and another Kiowa ahead to make a diversion before the main attack. They crept forward on their bellies, wary of dogs, their bows and arrows over their backs, their war hatchets at their belts, and their short spears in their hands. Yellow Horse and some others had muzzle-loading carbines, but they were slow and heavy; Sanjak put more trust in his bow, which was swift and sure. There was a wall running from the upper end of the village down to the river bed, but the main defense was a hedge of organ cactus, twice a man's height and almost impenetrable, stretching between the houses and the ridge. It would be possible, however, to break through at the gate if there was a distraction.

Sanjak and his companion crept around the end of the wall and, crawling along within its shadow, found the corral where the trade horses were held for sale. They slipped past the corral, saw that it was unguarded, and went on to the far side of the village. Here they found a hut with a pile of straw in the yard that suited their purpose. Shielded by his companion, Sanjak struck flint until he had a fire, lighted a tuft of straw, and thrust it into the pile. Quickly, but silently, they crept back by the way they had come.

It was only a moment before a cry arose in the air. At the same instant the fire, breaking through the straw, leaped in tongues of flame and threw a garish light upon the whole village. In the hot glare of the orange and blue flames crackling and breaking apart high in the air, the villagers could be seen; roused from their sleep, they rushed half-clad into the streets, some carrying buckets of water, others wailing helplessly and crowding the ways—among them old men, women, children, and nursing babies in their mothers' arms.

This was the moment for attack. However, the raiders' movements were hampered by the narrow streets, and they were divided in their goals. Some of the younger men, who had no squaws, were eager to capture Mexican girls, while older ones, more bloodthirsty from many battles, wanted mainly horses, and scalps for their belts. Among these latter was Sanjak. . . .

A Mexican appeared from around the corner with a musket in his hands. Sanjak's skin grew tense; blood lust took possession; before the Mexican could aim his weapon, Sanjak was upon him. He crushed the side of the man's skull with a blow of his war ax, and then with a swift, deft movement of his knife, lifted the bloody scalp.

There was clamor in the direction of the corral, and through the smoke-filled alleys Sanjak found his way there.

And then it was that he saw Running Wolf in trouble. Two men with machetes were attacking him, and he was defending himself with only his war hatchet. Behind him, crouching against the wall, with a baby in her arms, was the Woman.

"Kee-oo-wah!" shouted Sanjak. The war cry of his people would summon help; meanwhile, he threw himself upon the nearer of the villagers. The two turned upon Sanjak. Flailing him with their burnished cane knives, they forced him to the wall while he defended himself by parrying with his ax and feinting. The Mexicans pressed their advantage, and Sanjak, keeping his back to the wall, slowly retreated. He was not afraid; the Mexicans were not good at this work; in such a contest their steel blades were unequal to his war ax; but he was growing tired.

Smoke that had been drifting through the alley suddenly surged into a fog to burn the eyes and choke the lungs, forcing both attacker and attacked to the ground for air. Smoke was something neither machete nor war club could subdue.

The pall lasted but a moment and was followed by a reddish glare from the burning village. The two Mexicans had disappeared. And, as Sanjak discovered, so had Running Wolf and the Woman and her baby.

Sanjak reached the corral, but it was empty, and the fighting had died down. He could hear the yells of the band as they drove the herd toward the hills. He was weary now, and had the vague nausea that always came over him after a battle. The yelling grew faint, and there was a silence, broken only by a wailing from the village and the occasional cry of an owl.

He was suddenly affected by a deflation of spirit, a shrinking of self, a listlessness like that which comes from the loss of blood in battle; but Sanjak had been lucky, he had come out with mere scratches, no more than a wetness under the arm. Rousing himself, he hurried to overtake his companions. He did not like being alone just now; he did not feel fear, but a need to escape his mood.

He reached the rim from which he had looked down upon the village and from which the attack had been launched. A little farther beyond, he found his pony tethered. He came to the animal, mounted, and set out northward.

Aside from the single scalp he had taken, Sanjak was returning from the raid empty-handed. He thought of the horses he had missed, of the women he might have taken—of the Woman, rather, who crouched by the wall. He saw her round, ruddy face, and the great dark eyes filled with fright and with something more that he did not understand. He thought that she must have a husband somewhere. He wondered if the man had been killed in the raid. It did not matter. . . .

TWO

It was toward morning before Sanjak caught up with the band, riding hard to be sure of escaping pursuit. Presently he saw Running Wolf. He was leading a pony, and the Woman sat upon it. Her dress was torn and her brown legs bore welts and scratches; she had a serape loosely thrown about her shoulders, and she sat with head bowed, swaying awkwardly to the movement of the pony, as though at any moment she might fall. It was at at this moment that Sanjak first noted the object that later became for him what the Kiowas call *medicine*. It was on a chain about the Woman's neck, falling to the swell of her breasts—a silver figure of a man, his arms outstretched, fastened to a cross.

For a moment the silver image held his attention to the

exclusion of everything else. What did it mean? Was it, he thought, the Woman's medicine? If so, it had not been a very good medicine. Sanjak again felt the emptiness of spirit of the night before. Was it dissatisfaction that his hands were empty, that he was returning with neither horses nor woman? Something about the silver image troubled him, and he wondered whether it had value.

And then as Sanjak regained composure and his contemplation returned to the Woman on the pony, he became aware of an omission. He rode up to Running Wolf. Running Wolf was short and thick—for all that a marvelous horseman—and his face was mottled and marked from the smallpox, which had given him red, inflamed eyes with short vision. He also had a sickness that sometimes troubled him when he was astride.

"Where is the papoose?" Sanjak asked.

"It cried and would not silence when I spoke to it," responded Running Wolf, "and so I left it."

Sanjak became again the man of his people, with the concern for the community that was later to make him a chief. The Kiowas were not a numerous people. Too many of the squaws were barren, and the pox and the litter sickness took too many of those who were born.

"You should not have done so," he protested sharply. "We need papooses in the lodges. How can we stand against the Utes and the Osage if we do not have more men children? Was it a man child?"

"I think."

Sanjak saw the Woman stir within the blanket, and her head turn, and suddenly he was again aware of her eyes upon him. That she understood the Kiowa tongue was to be doubted, yet there was something of understanding and of appeal in her look as she turned to Sanjak.

"Where did you leave the baby?"

"In the cactus."

"Far?"

Running Wolf glanced at the sun, now disentangling itself

from the tree branches of the distant creek.

"About the setting of the Papoose."

The Papoose was the name in the Kiowa tongue of a constellation that shone in the summer night. Running Wolf thought of the pun and began to giggle.

"Big Papoose go behind the hills, little papoose go into the cactus. Ha! Ha!"

Sanjak was quite a joker himself, but now his humor failed.

He turned his pony's head on the trail and galloped off.

"Come back," shouted Running Wolf, alarmed. "You will never find it. Why do you seek it?"

But Sanjak had disappeared in the gray haze of the dawn, and Running Wolf, disquieted and humorless as he recalled how he had deserted Sanjak in the fight, lashed his pony and shouted angrily at his captive.

Sanjak did not know why he had returned to search for the Woman's infant. He thought of the constellation known as the Papoose. The stars shone as though they were the large and brilliant eyes of some being in the sky; Sanjak had often watched them as they moved across the black void of the heavens, and marveled at what held them there. Whose eyes were they that winked at him as he lay on the prairie at night? Often, when unable to sleep because of the majesty of the mood that struggled within him, Sanjak's thoughts pondered the number of eyes that looked down upon him, and asked which among them was the one that particularly held him in its gaze.

Of late, more than ever, these strange musings and swelling moods filled his soul, until at times he felt as though he would burst, so strongly did they struggle within him for release. And in some ways these moods now became connected with the infant, lying abandoned and bruised because in its ignorance it had dared give vent to its own hungers and moods, and had cried.

Despite his hunter's intuitions and his taught faculties, Sanjak thought it must be the Woman's medicine that led him to the seeming impossible, even for an Indian. For in the vast spaces of the desert he came to the very clump of mesquite and cactus into which Running Wolf had hurled the infant. There was no sound, no stirring, but Sanjak's eye caught the flutter of a wisp of cloth. Dropping from his mount and pressing in, he saw and retrieved the body.

The baby was dead. Sanjak looked for a moment at the bruised and swollen flesh, and then wrapped it carefully in its own blanket and in his own and mounted, and set off northward, bearing his burden—his only trophy of the raid.

He caught up with the raiding party that evening, encamped among the cottonwood, and silently presented his burden to the Woman, sitting apart from the fires, staring fearfully into the gloom. She took the baby to her bosom, removed the coverlet from its face, and gazed at it. Then she bowed her head and began a convulsive shuddering.

Two weeks later, they had crossed the Red River and were again in the Kiowa-Comanche country.

THREE

Sanjak sat in his lodge with his two squaws, the broad-faced Brown Berry and Bird-that-Sings, who was the older. The squaws were sisters. Loping Rabbit, Sanjak's brother, had paid twenty horses down to old Man-Standing-Up for Bird-that-Sings, but then had gone off with a war party against the Utes and had never returned. Man-Standing-Up insisted that Sanjak do a brother's duty by taking the girl, which he did, and a little afterward Brown Berry, whom he liked better, came to join them in the lodge. That was the way things were done in those days among the Kiowas and their brothers the Comanches.

Sanjak was content with the squaws. While he liked the council fire and council debate and the ceremonies of the Red

Leg Society, he also liked—at times more than anything else—to sit in his comfortable lodge and meditate or listen to the chatter of the women.

His was a large lodge of eighteen skins, and comfortably furnished with mattresses resting on raised frames with rawhide webbing and covered with buffalo robes. Sanjak's was the largest bed, set against the tepee wall that faced the opening. In parfleche bags hanging from the binding thongs of the wall poles were stored extra clothing, store-bought food, cooking and eating utensils, and an assortment of oddments—from some ancient Spanish gold coins to an antelope tooth. Dangling from the center, under the roof, was a bag tightly sewn and never opened, the contents of which Sanjak was completely ignorant. He had obtained it from a great medicine man of the Cheyennes, and he had been told it was a powerful medicine to protect the lodge, even as the lesser medicine he wore in a sealed leather sack suspended from his neck was his personal protection.

Bird-that-Sings, the talkative one, was recounting the news of the month past, as she had already done for several days. Sanjak was in a contented, happy mood.

"The trader Peacock came to the lodges with his wheeled wagon drawn by the white mules," she was saying. "He had new combs for the hair and beads, and—"

"Yes, so you have said—but no guns?"

"No guns. I tried to buy guns for you, but he said the soldiers had searched his wagon and had taken them away. To be sure, I myself searched his wagon while he slept, and I found none."

"Soldiers, you had not said so," commented Sanjak absently. "Where were they?"

"I did not wish you to start again on the warpath. They were peaceable, and they brought presents to the chiefs. They came from the place they call Belknap, and they made camp at the foot of the Wichitas, and there was some talk that they plan to make a fort there, to keep the Kiowas and the Comanches from going on raids into Texas and Mexico."

Sanjak suddenly laughed and pinched Bird-that-Sings.

"You talk too much. It makes you fearful," he chided.

"No, no. I speak truly. We shall have much trouble from the horse soldiers. They have a new kind of rifle that goes *bang, bang,* before you can say *bang, bang.*"

From one of the distant tepees came a sound that caught Sanjak's attention.

"You do not listen to me," complained the squaw.

"No, Little Bird," said Sanjak. "I must think upon all the foolishness you have told me," and pinching her again playfully, he arose and went out. The lodges stood along the creek bank for the space of a mile. It was late afternoon, and here and there families were gathered around the cooking pots, feasting on roast buffalo meat and chattering in subdued voices, but most of the fires had died down to ruddy coals. The still air among the cottonwoods was filled with the haze of smoke.

It was to one of the tepees midway of the camp and set somewhat apart that Sanjak had been drawn by the sounds he had heard. They now took on a different tone; they became a wail, and then a cry of protest, a growl from the throat of an Indian brave, a shout of defiance, and a yell that was unmistakably from Running Wolf. Suddenly a figure broke from the tepee and ran fleeing into the prairie.

Running Wolf appeared at the opening and started to pursue, but Sanjak had stepped forward, and Running Wolf caught himself.

"The Woman," remarked Sanjak easily, "is like the hare that would not be caught."

"The Mexican has a devil," growled Running Wolf, nursing his arm.

"Did she bite you?" asked Sanjak with great solemnity.

Running Wolf would not admit to such an indignity, but it was plain that he had not yet possessed his captive, and Sanjak did not press the point. Instead, he said, "Playing with the white man's cards is much more fun. I am looking for someone to challenge. Will you play?"

"I will find it fun," said Running Wolf.

Running Wolf was so eager for the game that he followed Sanjak.

"The Woman?" asked Sanjak.

"When she gets hungry, she will return."

Sanjak led Running Wolf to his tepee, collecting several idle braves as he went. He dispossessed the squaws, laid some sticks on the fire and blew them to life, and fetched forth a greasy deck of cards he had obtained from the trader Peacock on an earlier visit.

The cards recalled the trader to mind, and the thought in turn recalled Bird-that-Sings's chatter about his last visit. As he thumbed the cards, Sanjak now turned over in his mind the news Peacock had brought. It would not be good news that the soldiers were planning an encampment on the edge of the Kiowa-Comanche country. Every year there was news of some such move, each year a new encroachment on the hunting grounds of the tribe. This latest event was something that should be brought to the council fire, on which the wisdom of the chiefs and the elders should be heard.

"You mix the cards too much," laughed Crow Black, one of the onlookers. "Do you dream of honey or the sour grape?"—meaning of love or war.

"Neither, but of twenty ponies that Running Wolf shall win of me."

This was Sanjak's private joke with himself, for he had no intention of losing twenty ponies to Running Wolf, nor to anyone else; indeed, he was known as a highly successful gambler.

He dealt, and the cards went around. The game was one of their own invention, a highly elaborated imitation of an ill-remembered game that the trader had taught the Indians.

The news quickly spread that Sanjak and Running Wolf were playing at cards and that the stakes were running high. Running Wolf was a great boaster and had often celebrated his winnings. He would bet on anything—horses being his favorite, for he was a good judge of horseflesh, and he could almost name the swiftest horse by looking at it, or watching it move around its peg. But he was less adept at cards. Sanjak, who was his equal as a judge of horseflesh, was his better as a judge of men, but this was something he wisely kept to himself. For this reason he was good at cards, but he deprecated his successes and let it be known that they were happenstances entirely. The tepee was now crowded, but the braves were courteously silent, except for the grunts of triumph and disappointment among the partisans as the turns were won or lost.

There was no question of manipulating the cards, of trickery in dealing or shuffling, for cards were alien to the Indian culture, a novelty to which their hands, however skillful in hunt or war, never became accustomed. If there was skill, it was entirely in that profound art of reading the human heart, of recognizing the limits to which daring will carry a man, how far caution will draw him back. Sanjak was recognized as a skilled warrior who had the capacity to become a war chief; his leadership was due to his courage and skill and patience and zeal; but beyond those to his ability to measure the strength of his own forces, and to know where and how far they could be used. These in turn derived from his intuitive ability to perceive the temper of his adversaries, the strength of their fiber, the length to which their patience could be drawn, the mistakes they would make from excessive zeal.

A little pile of colored quills by Sanjak's thigh showed how much he was winning. Running Wolf's coppery skin glistened with sweat as his eyes grew beady. Sanjak arose and went to the tepee opening and gazed into the night. A pallor had appeared in the east, and the breeze was cool on the cheek.

"You do not leave the game now that you have won all my herd?" asked Running Wolf.

"No," replied Sanjak deliberately. "I listen to the sounds of the morning—the first bird calls, the papooses for the milk of their mothers, and the mournful sigh of one who has spent the night alone, who looks for her man's return."

Returning to the circle, he asked, "What do you say? Will you wager the Woman against your herd of horses that now are mine?"

"Take her," said Running Wolf, standing and shaking his great shoulders in fury. "Take her, for she is bad medicine. From the day I seized her in the raid, the black wolves of misfortune have hung about the tepee."

"I will not take her as a gift, but I will wager for her," said Sanjak. To take her without compensation might be unlucky. He sat down at the cards and began to deal. The men were silent, and the only sounds were the clap of hands as the cards were played, to signal a bid in which the fingers were lifted, and the grunts of the onlookers as this or that successful play was made. In the light of the glowing coals the sweating faces were like oiled copper, the eyes like the black mouth of the white man's rifle.

Suddenly Running Wolf stood up.

"Take the Woman!" he grunted.

"No," said Sanjak firmly. "But I will give you the horses for her. It is done." And he lifted his arm in the solemn gesture that confirmed the trade before all the witnesses.

And so the Woman passed into the hands of Sanjak.

FOUR

"You have a wildcat which you must not leave uncaged," Running Wolf had warned. Secretly he regretted giving up the Woman, for her very wildness and defiance challenged him, and he had told himself that one day he would take her, regardless of how she resisted. But it would have to be done carefully. Once when he had approached her she had seized a knife and dared him, and only by craft and professed submissiveness had he persuaded her to drop it.

Sometime during the night, while the game was on, the Woman had been driven by fear of the prowling wolves to return to the lodge. Finding Running Wolf absent, she had crept under a blanket next to Running Wolf's squaw and had slept. And now at Running Wolf's return with Sanjak she was awake, and she faced them again with her look of fear and defiance. She was, Sanjak noted, still in her Mexican dress, torn and soiled, with the image hanging from the chain about her throat; her hair was matted and fell to her shoulders, and her face was grimy.

She was, Sanjak noted further, not quite so tall as he, who was tall among the Kiowas, and she was slim like a poplar tree, not thick like the Kiowa women, and her eyes were of the color of the rock the white men burned to make fire.

"Come with me," he said to her quietly, in the measured tones he used when around the council fire he was asked to give his view on the grave issues of war and peace. He spoke in the commonly used Comanche dialect. The Woman gazed at him with an empty look of not understanding, and Sanjak explained with a gesture. She followed him.

Brown Berry and Bird-that-Sings, who had spent the night in the lodge of old Crooked Horse, had returned and were already busy, in their desultory way, with the work of the day—gathering wild honey and pounding jerked meat to make the winter supply of pemmican. They had already heard that Sanjak was bringing back the Mexican woman, or at least they showed no surprise at her appearance, but went on with their work. Brown Berry, however, seeing the Woman's condition, went to her parfleche bag and fetched a dress of hers with bead trimming, and a comb, and gave them to her. Neither had been used—Brown Berry was careless as to personal appearance, or indifferent. The Woman accepted them silently, went to one of the mattresses, and sat down.

Sanjak went out. It was a warm day, and he was tired from the long night at cards. He went to the tether line and, taking one of the ponies, rode far out into the prairie until he came to a grove of cottonwood. There he dismounted and sat in the grass to meditate but presently went to sleep.

When he returned toward evening, the Woman was helping the squaws cut up dried venison for the pot. She had a sharp knife in her hand. She was wearing the Indian dress of worked antelope skin that Brown Berry had given her. She had also been to the creek and bathed, for her face shone like copper, and her hair, blue-black like her eyes, was combed and braided. At Sanjak's entrance she laid down the knife and returned to the mattress on which she had sat in the morning. Drawing a blanket about her, she regarded Sanjak watchfully, assessing his intentions, fearful apparently but with a kind of passivity born of exhaustion.

Sanjak noticed again the cross with the man on it and wondered again at the kind of medicine it might be. The image—the man on the cross—troubled him, and he recalled how he had been led to find the Woman's baby in the cactus. Was it as powerful as the medicine he wore on a string around his neck, which had protected him from harm in so many raids, or the medicine that hung from the lodge pole and protected his household?

His medicine was not all-powerful, as Brown Berry indirectly reminded Sanjak that evening as he lay down beside her in the dark. The Woman sat crouched on the farthest mattress, saying nothing.

"You do not make love to the Mexican?" Brown Berry whispered.

"No, little one. I am content."

"We give you no papooses. She is fruitful. She has given birth. You may make love to her."

"I am content," said Sanjak shortly. "Let us sleep."

The next day Brown Berry, who was the more tender and affectionate of the two squaws, returned to the subject.

"You don't want the Woman? You keep her for ransom?"

"Maybe," said Sanjak. "When the trader comes, maybe we make a good bargain." He pinched Brown Berry playfully. "Too many squaws now. Squaws talk too much. No time to think of council, or Great Spirit."

"Papooses plenty fun. We should have papooses."

"Maybe I can trade her for one."

Sanjak was not speaking truthfully, for he was not yet ready to surrender the Woman.

"We must give her a name," he said.

Looking at her now, as she bent over the fire silently stirring the pot, he spoke.

"Blossoming Bough," he said, pointing to her. The name seemed appropriate, because from the moment she entered his tepee Sanjak was aware that something new had entered, something more than a person, something he could not define, but was like the scent of the purple bunch flower that wafted across the prairie, a something you could sense but could not quite grasp.

But an Indian name did not seem quite right for an alien woman, and Sanjak thought further. Then, as out of the darkness of a mystery, came the name *Ileeta*, a word without meaning to him, but all the more meaningful because, like the Woman, it came out of the darkness of mystery. Ileeta he would call her. Ileeta.

The Woman gave no sign of understanding. Sanjak repeated the name several times, but the Woman merely looked at him. He grew urgent to possess her. Finally his patience gave way, and his face grew dark with anger. He took up his quirt to compel her response—but hesitated. It would do no more good than it had with Running Wolf. He dropped the quirt and strode from the lodge. . . .

It was Sanjak's way, when he wanted to make love to one of his squaws, to tickle their feet by way of beginning. This would make them squirm and giggle—particularly Bird-that-Sings—and put them in good humor, and warmed them so that they squirmed the more when he took them in his embrace, and lovemaking was all the more delightful.

That evening he began tickling the feet of Bird-that-Sings. The squaw squirmed and giggled, and held out her arms, but Sanjak ignored her invitation. He was watching Ileeta, who in turn was watching his antics with her veiled eyes. Picking up a reed, he twirled it, pretending to be thinking, but slyly began to tickle Ileeta's ankle. She jerked away.

His advances again rebuffed, Sanjak abruptly rose and left the lodge to contain his mood. He walked out into the prairie, far away from the camp until he was alone under the arching,

star-filled sky. Squatting in the grass, he began to croon, in a
quavering voice, a song he improvised,

> *Wah loo eeta mi ha loo*
> *Bittah een par ano hee*
> Say, O Wind beneath the Stars,
> How close You are to Me;
> Yet where You are
> And where am I—I know not. . . .

PART

2

Ileeta

ONE

The Comanche war chief Tall Man paid a visit to the Kiowa encampment with his warrior band and assembled the Red Leg Society. Tall Man was a good raider—a bold fighter, reckless almost and not too shrewd, tall but too heavy from much buffalo fat and pemmican, and needing a big horse to carry him, good-natured when not aroused.

The braves conferred in the open prairie, in a circle around a small fire, while the pipe was passed around.

"You have heard the news?" Tall Man began.

"That the white men have begun warring among themselves?"

"That."

Tall Man said nothing for a moment, and drew on the pipe,

which had come to him from Sanjak.

"All the white warriors are hurrying away to battle. The forts at Belknap and Phantom Hill—empty. It is a good time to take horses and cattle."

Sanjak's eyes had a question in them.

"Almost," added Tall Man, noting the question.

"I hear."

"We need not go so far as Mexico. Plenty of cattle and horses below Red River. Many buyers up north. I know a settlement where there are much cattle easily to be taken."

"I will wait a while," said Sanjak, speaking for himself.

Tall Man said nothing for a moment, then picked up a handful of dust and ran it through his fingers. Yellow Horse, leader of the Red Legs, turned to Sanjak for counsel.

Sanjak shook his head in dubiety.

"You have no desire?" asked the Comanche Tall Man.

"Yes, but there is much work to be done."

This was a euphemism, but not entirely. When not raiding or hunting—or contemplating the stars—Sanjak was busy making arrows, of which his were the straightest and best balanced in the entire band, made of the finest seasoned ash and *bois d'arc* and which he sometimes sold for a good price. He would not allow the squaws to help in this work, for much of the excellence he attributed to his medicine, which he would take from around his neck when he worked and hang it in front of the wood. He also had a number of traps along the creek, for pelts of beaver and raccoon were in good demand, and he deigned at times to help his squaws stretch soaked rawhide for the parfleche bags, since it took strong arms for that work. Some of the warriors joked with him about his women's work—but not much, for they respected his fighting ability, and they knew also that Sanjak could be aroused, and when aroused was hard to quiet.

Since the coming of the Woman, however, he had spent less time in the lodge, for Ileeta was still distrustful of him, and watched him warily when he was around. She was learning the language, and would converse with the squaws, and showed an interest in learning Indian handicraft—and on her part had taught Bird-that-Sings certain Mexican arts of cooking and how to fashion the trader's cloth into comfortable garments. All of this Sanjak had noted with satisfaction. Under her influence also Brown Berry took better care of herself, combing her hair more frequently, and bathing. Sanjak particularly liked the stews Ileeta made in the Mexican fashion flavored with certain herbs that she gathered on the prairie.

"We can capture more women maybe. That is good for the lodge, good for ransom," Tall Man was saying.

Three women had been taken on the earlier raid into Mexico, two of them by the Comanches. One of these had subsequently been killed, the other had fled and had been found dead, washed up on a sandbar in the Red River, in which she had apparently drowned.

"Sanjak has plenty squaws," spoke up Running Wolf, with a forced laugh, for he had never forgotten his loss of the Woman. "He has become a squaw man."

Sanjak made no comment to this, but inwardly he knew that Running Wolf was no longer his friend.

"It is not good to raid into Texas," he declared and then, rising to his feet, began to speak.

"It is true," he began slowly, choosing his words, but gathered them as he went along, "that the white men are now warring among themselves. But because they are warring, they are fashioning for themselves many more of the iron pieces that utter fire. They are making new kinds also that can speak faster. Beyond that, many who were content to keep to the lodge with their squaws and till the soil or tend their herds are now becoming warriors, either going off to war or guarding their belongings about their lodges.

"The white men have offered to smoke the peace pipe with us. They do not want to quarrel with us while warring among themselves. They offer good bounty if we agree to peace. Have they not done so with our kinsmen the Cheyennes and Arapahoes?"

Sanjak referred to the recent treaty by which the two tribes were to receive a yearly payment in silver dollars and freedom from trespass in their hunting grounds on the Smoky River.

Running Wolf now stood up in opposition to Sanjak.

"Sanjak is a noted warrior, and a wise man in council," he began, "but he sits in the moonlight and converses with the Great Spirit too much for a man of the trail and a man of the warpath. This is the talk of a fledgling, of one who has not yet left the nest, a stripling who has not yet donned war paint— not the speech of a man whose warbonnet already carries a double fringe."

It was not seemly in council to attack another warrior's qualities, his bravery or lack of it, his skill or lack of foresight. It was enough to consider the wisdom he uttered, whether it be wisdom or no. Sanjak knew now with certainty that Running Wolf was no longer a friend, more, that now he was an enemy. He ignored the barb but laid it away in memory.

"Consider the buffalo," Sanjak resumed, "that continue to graze while one of their herd is brought low by the silent arrow, that are aroused only by the smell of the hunter or the thunder of the hunter's gun. The people of Texas are not like the buffalo. They are more like the antelope, with both ears and eyes upon the enemy, wary and ready to leap. Or like the bobcat guarding her young, ready to pounce before the hunter is aware.

"The old men of the tribe remember the days—not many winters back—when the Comanches and Kiowas hunted and camped in the land of the Texans. The chiefs were invited to council with their leaders. We were at peace, and the peace pipe was being smoked. But Chief Gray Wolf had brought his war hatchet, hung from his belt under his robe. You all know the story. His robe fell from his shoulder. At the sight of the hatchet the white men took fright. They became like the prairie rat when taken. They became like one whose locks and feathers have been set afire, like men drunk on peyote. At once they fell upon the chiefs, none of whom was armed except Gray Wolf, and all were killed. It was then that the

Comanches were driven north across the Red River and forbidden to return. The Texans fear us. Let us leave them alone. There are horses still in Mexico."

All this was given thought as the pipe passed around.

The council broke up inconclusively. Some saw the wisdom of Sanjak's counsel, but it was spring, the ancient time of warfare, when the ponies were lean and hardy for travel, not yet time for the buffalo hunt, and many of the braves had spent their captured wealth and needed more booty. Several of the Red Legs joined Tall Man's party, but Yellow Horse was among those who accepted Sanjak's view.

Three weeks later the war party returned with three of the band wounded and one dead, over whom there was great keening for a week.

"Tall Man said for us to follow the wire hung on poles," Running Wolf explained, "that it would lead to a place of many lodges and much cattle. But some medicine had warned the white man, and before we reached the place, they fell upon us with many guns, and we escaped only because our horses were faster."

TWO

The Nut Eaters—the Kiowa band to which Sanjak and his people belonged—were now camped along the Arkansas where grew many of the edible nuts that gave the band its name. Among these were the pecan, black walnut, and hazel. These were gathered by the squaws and blended with persimmon and berry pulp into a paste that was much in demand among the Indians and even among some of the white residents in the Indian country.

The camp lay not far from the trail that the white men made in their journeys to the Great Water to the west. There were fewer wagon trains on that trail now, and the great chiefs of the Comanches and Kiowas had agreed with the chiefs of the army not to molest those who passed in exchange for restraint by the army.

With these agreements and the white men's preoccupations with their own quarrel, and after the disaster of Tall Man's raid into Texas, there followed peaceful days for the band, and pleasant hours in Sanjak's lodge.

Ileeta had gradually adjusted to her life as a captive. Though Sanjak respected her person, she was seldom out of his ken, and for her part she no longer watched him warily as earlier but accepted her lot as a member of the lodge, doing her share of the work and sometimes carrying on a lively conversation with the squaws—though usually reticent when Sanjak was around.

She did not adorn herself as did certain women of the tribe who courted many men; rather she avoided attention. Sanjak noted that she kept her face washed and her clothes clean and her hair combed more frequently than the squaws. It amused him to watch her braid her hair, for this was man's custom among the Kiowas. Women cropped their hair short to hang just below the ears and seldom combed it.

One day Bird-that-Sings hurried into the lodge from the creek, where she had been gathering wild plums for pemmican.

"Two wagons drawn by mules come in the distance. They are the wagons of the trader, Peacock."

The trader usually made his visits during the fall and spring, for this was after the pelts taken during the preceding season had been well dressed and tanned. As the word spread through the camp, the squaws abandoned their work and the children their play to watch the wagons draw near.

Sanjak was in his lodge. Brown Berry and Bird-that-Sings went out to see the trader. Ileeta glanced at Sanjak, then went to her mattress, where she drew a doeskin coverlet around her and sat immobile. Sanjak said nothing, but presently he arose and went out.

The trader had drawn up his wagons at a respectful distance, and his men, of whom there were four, were making camp. There were two wagons each covered with tarpaulins stretched over big hoops and drawn by four mules. Peacock and his wagoners were all heavily armed with short guns on their hips and Henry rifles leaning nearby against the wheels.

When they had tethered the mules, made camp, and lighted a fire, Peacock walked toward the lodges, holding his arms aloft in a sign of peaceful greeting. He had left his weapons behind.

The elders of the band, Sanjak among them, now took notice and went out in a group to welcome him. After greetings in both sign language and Comanche, they squatted in the prairie and smoked a pipe around, after which Peacock announced his readiness for business, inquiring if there were fur pelts or dressed skins or bead work for sale.

The traders who visited the Indian encampments were usually hearty and outgoing, of the kind to serve confidence and custom, rough-clad and rough-spoken men who liked Indians, understood them, and enjoyed being among them. Peacock was of a different temperament, with moods not easily fathomable, sometimes gay with a wry humor, sometimes aloof with a tinge of what might be bitterness or resentment, so that one might wonder whether he really liked Indians, whether he did not secretly fear them. He was a tall man, thin as a travois pole, with watchful eyes that flitted about like a sparrow hopping among the droppings of a buffalo. He laughed a great deal while trading, as though it were a matter of amusement, laughed even when a piece of crockery was accidentally broken. Like the Kiowas, he liked to play practical jokes, as when, so it was said, he filled the hat of one of the Caddoes with ants, hidden behind the sweat band. The Caddo was one of the settlement Indians who walked the white man's road and wore white man's dress. Peacock would never have dared such a pleasantry with a Kiowa.

The Kiowas were not particularly fond of Peacock, but he was tolerated, for he was a useful go-between in ransoming captives and selling the horses they captured on their raids. The army tolerated him for the same reason; it was cheaper to buy back the horses and the captives than to send expeditions.

He remained with the band a week, making good business buying pelts and buffalo robes and selling copperware and printed cloth and cutlery. Sanjak offered to barter some of his ponies for one of the new Henry rifles, a few of which he was certain the trader had hidden in his wagons. But Peacock denied having any, and Sanjak left off and turned further dealings over to the squaws. He did not care for trafficking; he grew weary at haggling for a price; he could understand coined money but not the new pieces of paper the trader insisted on giving instead.

A little later, seeing Sanjak among the braves watching from a distance, the trader set one of his wagoners over his goods while he left and called to Sanjak.

"You like a good, first-class Henry rifle?" he asked cautiously when they were alone. "Never used?"

"How much?"

"What you pay?" adopting the laconic Kiowa manner of speaking.

"Twenty horses."

The trader gave a low cackling laugh.

"Horses plentiful. What else?"

"Thirty horses."

"Horses too plentiful. Grass not plentiful. How I feed thirty horses?"

Sanjak had a superb buffalo robe, beautifully worked with curious designs by Bird-that-Sings. He offered that. Peacock demurred.

Sanjak wanted the rifle very much. He could almost feel the smooth cold metal under his hands.

"What you want?" he asked.

"I tell you," said Peacock at last, with a laugh. "I have need for a good Mexican woman. I hear you have one that you hold for ransom here. I'll take the Mexican for the rifle—and I'll do more. I'll throw in a box of cartridges."

Sanjak looked at the trader from under lidded eyes.

"Why you want Mexican? Nobody wants Mexican woman. Maybe I can find you white woman."

43

Peacock held his hand beside his mouth so that his speech would not carry—unlikely in any case to be heard the hundred yards distance from the lodges—and dropped his voice.

"I'll tell you," he said with a low cackle of a chuckle. "Mexican women much prized in the army camps in Missouri. That's why I can give you good money and another box of cartridges."

"Soldiers like Mexican women?" asked Sanjak, knowing very well for what purpose. "Maybe two Henry rifles?"

Peacock's voice now became a sort of squeak.

"You good trader," he commented. "Two rifles with cartridges."

"How you know I have a Mexican woman?" demanded Sanjak suddenly.

"Why, why," hemmed the trader. "So I heard."

"You hear much. Have you seen any Mexican woman in our camp?"

"They say—"

"Who say?"

Peacock now began to stroke his mustache either to regain or to affect composure. He knew the temper of the Kiowas and of Sanjak in particular. Sanjak's voice began to growl.

"No Mexican woman for sale. You understand. You no see Mexican woman. You tell no one you see. Understand?"

"Yes, yes," squeaked Peacock, with a cackling giggle. "No Mexican woman. I have seen none."

Satisfied and mollified, Sanjak now said,

"Now I sell you horses and take much trade goods. You show me."

Together they went to the second wagon, where Peacock kept his finer merchandise, which Sanjak now pawed over until he found what pleased him—a large twist of tobacco, a bolt of brightly colored calico, another of good woolen, a Bowie knife, several strands of colored glass beads, a fan comb, and a looking glass.

"How much?" he asked.

"Five horses," said Peacock hesitantly, since two would have been enough.

"You come tomorrow to my tether and take," said Sanjak, indifferent as to the trader's choice.

He gathered up his purchases and returned to his lodge. There he deposited them on a buffalo robe spread on the floor. As the two squaws squealed with delight over this or that trinket, Sanjak picked up the comb and mirror and silently laid them in Ileeta's lap. She did not move, or seem to notice, but later, as Sanjak sat cross-legged on his mattress smoking, he saw Ileeta pick up the glass and examine her face, then smooth some strands of hair that had escaped from one dark braid.

Sanjak was pleased.

THREE

After presenting Ileeta with the trinkets he had purchased, Sanjak went far out into the prairie, where a lone cottonwood spread a broad shade. Here he sat while an afternoon breeze blew, and he listened to the voices of the earth and sky about him—the rustle of leaves overhead, the call of a quail in the nearby distance, and the hum of bees in the tall sweet grass. He had no thoughts; he simply listened to hear, perchance, the voice of the Great Spirit speaking to him. He was not a man to think of the future. The present offered plenty to occupy his thoughts—and there were memories, mostly inchoate, mostly pleasant, of a hearty meal of venison, of amblings on the prairie, of nights in the lodge warmed by his squaws. There were also some unpleasant memories, like the days he spent in the white man's stockade, and the raid on Santa Rosa when he lost the Woman to Running Wolf. . . . Sanjak did not dwell on unpleasant memories, he preferred the pleasanter, but the thought of Running Wolf stirred dark designs and with them an unpleasant sense of dilemma. . . .

He rose suddenly and returned to the lodges. It was growing late in the day, and as he passed the camp of the trader, he noted that one wagon loaded with pelts had already been covered with tarpaulin and strapped ready, and that the other was being loaded for travel.

In his lodge he found Ileeta working some soft deerskin into a shirt for him, and he was suddenly pleased and pained. He beckoned to her to come with him.

She came, docilely enough, and he led her away from the camp along the creek bank, until they came to a grove on a grassy knoll where they could see the sun setting in the west, like a great chief going down to his last rest, his head haloed with his warbonnet of many colors, and his spear sparkling and shield flamboyant.

"Let us sit," he said.

"You like the glass?" Sanjak asked presently, keeping his speech to monosyllables and words that Ileeta understood.

"Yes."

"The Yankee trader wishes to take you," Sanjak said. "Would you like to go?"

"Where to?"

"To the white settlement—where you find people like you."

"No," said Ileeta shortly. "I am Mexican." She was sitting, looking toward the west, toward the setting sun, the rays of which lighted her face and filled it with golden sheen. To Sanjak, looking at her, the thought came that she might be the wife of the Sun Chief.

"White people, Mexican people, all the same."

"No, not all the same."

"Same tribe, different breed. Both different from Kiowas."

Ileeta was silent.

"Were you afraid of the Yankee?"

"No."

"The Yankee offered a good price," said Sanjak.

Ileeta shuddered, as though the wind were suddenly cold, and Sanjak lifted his hand to feel its direction, but there was no wind.

"I do not love the Yankee," she said.

"Good," exclaimed Sanjak. "He would do you ill. He would sell you to a house of love."

Suddenly Ileeta was in tears and was lying crouched on the grass sobbing into her arms. Sanjak regarded her in perplexity.

Kneeling and bending over, he asked, "You want me to take you back to Mexico? Say so, and Sanjak will take you home."

"No, no, no," wailed Ileeta, and Sanjak was even more puzzled. He thought that perhaps she had not understood him, that he was threatening her for her tears, so he spoke again:

"No tears," he said gruffly. "Sanjak will take you back to Mexico."

At this Ileeta turned and looked up at him, eyes large and filled at once with wonder and despair.

"Why?" she asked.

Sanjak did not know why, and he felt a strange embarrassment at the question.

"To stop your crying," he said. "To whom do you belong? To whom shall I take you?"

"I belong to no one. No place to take me to," said Ileeta solemnly, despondently. "Take me and kill me."

"No papa? No mama?"

"No."

"You have no man?"

Ileeta avoided the question. "Running Wolf kill my baby," she said. "Nobody belongs to me."

"Where is your husband?" Sanjak demanded.

Ileeta was silent, then burst out,

"No husband. Never a husband."

Sanjak reflected on this. Suddenly he understood.

"Ha! Ha! Everybody your husband."

Ileeta shrugged her shoulders.

"Why had you no husband?" he asked.

"Papa killed, mama killed when I was little, and no one left to make marriage for me."

"Who would ransom you then?"

"No one. No one in village would pay ransom. No money."

Sanjak recalled that there was little wealth in the village. Her dress, he recalled also, had been gaudy but wretched and patched. For ornament the only thing she wore was the curious medicine that hung from a chain about her throat—the cross with the outstretched figure fastened to it, a thing of silver and of some worth, but little.

"Then you stay with me," announced Sanjak.

"No! I kill myself," announced Ileeta, suddenly sitting up and looking very stern.

"Ha! Ha!" laughed Sanjak. For some reason it struck him as funny, and for some reason his laughing brought a smile of amusement to Ileeta's face.

"You like hunting?" he changed the subject. "There will be a big buffalo hunt soon. Would you like to go?"

"I don't know," said Ileeta. "I never been hunting."

"You will like. Plenty to do, plenty to eat. Much running and chasing."

"I will see."

The sun had set now, and the light was fading from the sky, and a yellow moon was caught among the tree branches. Sanjak looked at the yellow moon, and presently he began to laugh, noiselessly, to himself. It was a laughter of joy. He felt very good, very pleased with life, with the good things of life. What else could a man ask for than what he had? He felt his manhood rising strong within him, like the sap when it fills the maple and the willow causing the skin of the tree to swell and to ooze sweetness.

Presently Ileeta said to him, "You have been good to me."

Now the word for "good" in the Kiowa tongue meant many

things. If the spore were plentiful, that was good. If the winter was mild, that was good. It was good to take a scalp, whether the hair came from the living or the dead victim. If you could trip your opponent in a wrestling match, that was good, and it was good to kill your squaw if she misbehaved. It was good to kill the man with whom she misbehaved, that is, if the man's family or society were not more powerful than your own. It was good sometimes to consult the council before doing such a deed, but sometimes it was good not to do so, but to take one's vengeance in any case. It was also good to take vengeance, though good in varying degrees. It was not good to allow one's enemy to escape, nor was it good to let babies cry. Besides these things, there were some new things that were good, such as the brown water that the traders sometimes sold, and the white man's firearms.

What Ileeta meant, therefore, when she said that Sanjak was good to her, was more than Sanjak could understand. What had he done for her that was good? Perhaps what he had done was very bad. It was not well to trust the notions of what was good to another not of the tribe, certainly not a white man, nor a Mexican. They said of many things that they were good, which to the eyes of the Kiowa were very bad. They thought it was good to hunt the buffalo for his tongue, or mayhap for his hide, which to the Kiowas was not good but very bad. They thought it was good to stay in one place and to live in a house that was all closed, which to the Kiowa, if not bad, was at least very foolish. They thought that much clothes upon the back was good, and tight leg coverings, and they thought it was good to cover the buttocks, whereas every Kiowa knew that it was most undignified to cover the buttocks, and besides, very hard on the cloth one used for the purpose.

"How?" he asked.

Ileeta hesitated. Finally,

"You are like a Christian to me."

"How?" asked Sanjak, puzzled. The word was not unfamiliar to him, for he had heard it in both Spanish and English, but he had little idea what it meant.

"You act as Jesus says for us to act. You do not beat me; you feed me."

"Who is Jesus?"

"This."

She held out her medicine—the cross with the man upon it.

Sanjak laughed. He was very careful about the spirits, and he was not laughing from irreverence, if he knew what irreverence meant. He was laughing because he knew the nature and use of medicines. They were good to bring the game and to give warning of the enemy and to strengthen the arm in battle, but they did not talk, nor did they tell you to feed your enemy, or not to beat a woman.

"Your medicine talks to you?" he asked.

Ileeta removed it from around her neck and held it out to him. Sanjak took it and now examined it carefully. It was much worn, but the general outline was plain. The man appeared to be in pain, which to a Kiowa was something not to be shown. Moreover, he had been nailed to the cross through the hands and through the feet. Someone had counted coup upon him, and he had been taken prisoner, and presumably his scalp would next be taken. There was nothing good about being a captive—certainly not for a medicine. How could a medicine be of any good to one when he was nailed and helpless and bleeding? It was very strange.

This was not the first cross Sanjak had seen, of course, but now that he was a man with two squaws and given more to meditation and contemplation upon the decisions of life, this was something to think about. What good was there in this figure?

It was plain that this medicine would say that it was not good to beat or to be beaten, though Sanjak would agree with neither. Sometimes it was good to be beaten, as when one had fallen into the river through the ice, or when one had the toothache or the pains in the back, or the fever; and also during the Sun Dance it was very good to be beaten, for then one saw visions—and besides, beating made one strong, and ready for the battle.

THE KIOWA

Sanjak looked again at Ileeta. He could hardly see her now, for the moonlight fell through the leaves in a mottled fashion, and all he could see was her form, dark upon the grass, and her eyes, which seemed to be glowing from their own light and were gazing at him steadily and solemnly. Suddenly Sanjak felt very happy, as when he had won his manhood and had been allowed to go on his first hunt, and again as when he had first counted coup upon an enemy, and as when he had killed his first buffalo. He began to sing, a joyous song, crooning as he improvised:

> *Ho yo, a he ah ye oh ho*
> *Enewahto anehanyah ki-ya-ki.* . . .
> The white owl sings in the night;
> The wind blows through the cottonwood;
> And the little white pebbles lie very still
> Beneath the rushing of the stream. . . ."

In his sudden gaiety he leaned over and began to tickle the soles of Ileeta's feet. She laughed and stretched out her foot, and in doing so turned over in the grass, lying upon her back, and her eyes laughing up at his. Sanjak crept a little nearer to her feet and tickled the other, while he laughed and sang, and then Ileeta's ankles.

Suddenly he was still, for a reason he knew not, and Ileeta was looking at him, and there was a sudden mingling of apprehension and expectancy in her eyes. Her lips had parted, and Sanjak waited, and it seemed to him that he was waiting for one of the stars to come and speak to him. There were words from Ileeta's lips, and they were,

"You are good to me, Sanjak."

Ileeta extended her arms, and Sanjak bent his head to hers. . . .

FOUR

The leaves of the sumac along the creek banks were turning to crimson, those of the aspen to yellow, and the buffalo grass to silver gray. The days grew shorter and the nights cooler, and the fur of the game was growing thick and soft. It was time for the fall buffalo hunt. Old Cow-with-a-Hump, the sage and medicine man, and keeper of the tribal calendar stick, had consulted the signs and had announced the day and the direction. The whole band struck camp and moved out southward toward the bottoms, where the buffalo herds were now grazing. Elsewhere throughout the Plains, other tribes and other bands were also in movement—but carefully avoiding the preserves assigned by tradition and usage to each.

In striking camp—in stripping the lodge poles of their

buffalo hide covering, folding them and lashing them to a travois made of the lodge poles themselves, binding and lashing the household gear to another—in all this Ileeta did her share of the work, taking her place as an equal with the two squaws, yet modestly as the least in rank. She did her work pleasantly and conversed amiably with the two, but in few words with Sanjak—in the manner of one with whom one has a perfect understanding. Bird-that-Sings and Brown Berry comprehended the new status Ileeta now held in the lodge—a status they accepted without question, though the garrulous Bird-that-Sings could sometimes be sharp-tongued and was inclined to scold Ileeta when through lack of skill or familiarity her bindings slipped. Ileeta took these rebukes without demur, and Sanjak noted her forbearance as he noted also her capacity for tenderness, which was different from that of Brown Berry. But how and in what way he could not say, for these things were still alien to his curiosity. He only knew that, content as he was with Brown Berry and Bird-that-Sings, he preferred Ileeta's company, and on the trail he had her ride by his side.

"Come with me," he said to her one morning and, giving his palomino the rein, set off across the plain.

Ileeta rode well, Sanjak noted with pleasure and recalled that she had grown up in horse country in Mexico. Together they rode far out across the rolling countryside out of sight of the caravan stretched along the trail.

"You like riding?" Sanjak asked. While he could rise to effective speech in council, in conversation generally he was laconic, and in addressing those like Ileeta whose understanding of the Kiowa tongue was imperfect, his habit was to speak in monosyllables.

"I like riding with you," responded Ileeta, her face flushed and her eyes shining with pleasure.

"You are good to me," she added.

"Good to everybody," responded Sanjak. He laughed and added, "Except enemies. Why do you all the time say, 'good to me'?"

"Why you tell me?" he repeated as they slowed their mounts to a walk.

"Because I like you. I will always like you." She was silent, and then burst out with, "I like you so—I give my life for you."

"No, no," cried Sanjak, alarmed, and reining up. "You must not say so. You must not talk so. You live, I live." These were feelings he did not understand.

A startled prairie hare with long mule ears leaped from the grass and went bounding across the prairie until it reached what it evidently regarded a safe distance, and then sat on its haunches, its ears pricked like moving sentinels. Sanjak was at once diverted.

Drawing an arrow from his quiver and fitting it, he exclaimed,

"Sanjak great hunter. Best in tribe. Watch."

"No, no!" cried Ileeta, terrified.

"No?" asked Sanjak incredulously.

"Why do you kill the rabbit, which you do not eat? We go after buffalo, no? Buffalo good for food, for clothes."

"Good!" exclaimed Sanjak. "But just the same I show you."

Replacing his arrow and unstringing his bow and lashing it, he rode slowly and quietly toward where the rabbit sat watchful. Just as he drew near, the rabbit leaped and bounded across the prairie. At the same instant Sanjak gave his well-trained mount the rein and galloped in pursuit. At the moment he was almost upon his quarry, the hare turned abruptly and in long leaps bolted in another direction. Sanjak wheeled his mount and was again in pursuit. Again the hare eluded him by quick turning—a maneuver in which it had the advantage. Presently, however, the pony's strength prevailed, and as it came alongside the hare Sanjak leaped and, falling full on the ground, seized it in his strong hands.

He grasped it by the feet and brought it triumphantly to Ileeta.

"Sanjak great hunter," he shouted joyfully, and let out a Kiowa war cry. "No one else in band, no one else in tribe, can catch game like Sanjak." He added as an afterthought, "No one has such good pony as Sanjak."

He held out the animal to Ileeta.

"See, I do not kill the rabbit. Are you pleased?"

Ileeta laughed with joy, and love brimmed in her eyes.

"Sanjak is a great hunter," she replied. "Sanjak is good to the rabbit. Sanjak is good to Ileeta. Now give the rabbit its freedom."

Solemnly Sanjak loosed the animal's feet and set it down, and immediately it bounded away—but not far, just beyond bowshot, where it again sat, its ears pricked, while it no doubt meditated the sky, and life, and the mystery of grace.

As for Sanjak, he was in a mixed mood. He was content with Ileeta but puzzled at her strange way of thinking. It was good to kill the buffalo—but bad to kill a rabbit—that was beyond him. Yet, as he puzzled, he was more and more subdued by Ileeta and wanted more and more to enter into the springs of her nature.

FIVE

Sanjak was sitting before his lodge in the crisp air and brilliant sunlight of autumn, fashioning arrows to replace those spent in the hunt. Jerky was drying on the line for the winter, and Brown Berry and Bird-that-Sings were pounding pemmican for the larder. Ileeta was sitting by Sanjak's side watching him work and helping him by handing him the feathers for the wings.

Those were pleasant days, and the Kiowa camp echoed with the sounds of play and work. The fall hunt had been good, and everywhere, on lines strung between saplings, strips of meat were drying. Outside the lodges, which stretched a great distance along the creek bank, squaws were scraping the freshly flayed hides stretched and held on the ground by pegs; others were baking sweet cakes of crushed mesquite beans and buffalo marrow, while the young girls of the band in their long doeskin shifts and doeskin boots ran errands, cutting firewood and fetching water. On the open field beyond, young braves were practicing horsemanship and the use of lance and bow from a galloping pony; and one chief was beating a drum and calling for a war party to attack the insolent Utes.

Sanjak was content, and more so as he let his eyes travel toward Ileeta. The Mexican woman had acquired a preferred status in the lodge. It was one that the two squaws had tacitly conceded, and Sanjak marveled at their compliance, pleased with himself and with the tranquility of his household, not aware yet that there might be another cause than himself for the deference shown to Ileeta.

Considering his household of three women dwelling in comparative harmony, he thought of the case of Crooked Nose and his squaw Willow Tree. Crooked Nose was an ungainly man with a vile breath and uneven temper; it was not unexpected that Willow Tree, who loved adornment, would be taking lovers and that now she had eloped with a wandering Ute. The taking of lovers was nothing much—the Kiowa and Comanche women had a great freedom in these matters—but relations with the Utes had never been friendly, there was periodic warring over hunting grounds or other disputes and offenses, and Crooked Nose had gathered his relatives and pursued the elopers. He had returned with the Ute's scalp and his errant squaw, whom he had marched from lodge to lodge, all the while beating her with a thong until her shoulders were bare and bloody and her shrieks filled the camp.

That was a proper happening in Sanjak's view. A man's dignity was important—more important than the size of his lodge or the number of ponies on his line—and offended dignity was to be avenged. Half the tribal quarrels and warfare arose, in fact, less over property—what was property to a nomadic race of men who roamed the vast plains as their own?—than over affronts to pride and dignity.

Yet the thought of the woman being beaten troubled Sanjak. A woman was a man's property—but not with Sanjak. At least he had never had to assert his right of property. Perhaps because his right had never been challenged. Neither Brown Berry nor Bird-that-Sings—both broad-faced, placid-eyed, and plump—were the kind to draw or be drawn by the wandering eye. Ileeta was of a different mold from that of Willow Tree. There was no woman in the camp with such unblemished face, with such glowing eyes, with such sycamore form, such antelope grace—but Ileeta, either from timidity or reserve, kept a downcast eye in the presence of the camp braves. She never left the lodge for any distance except in the company of one or the other squaw. She particularly avoided being seen by Running Wolf, and on one or two occasions when he suddenly appeared, her skin, normally the color of autumn grass, paled and fear filled her eyes.

Sanjak's hand, as he recalled these incidents and meditated on their meaning, had grown still, a half-fashioned shaft in his fingers. Ileeta touched him lightly on the arm.

"You are tired? You wish to rest your head in my lap?"

"That would be good, my prairie dove, but I am not tired."

"Then of what do you think?"

Sanjak was evasive. In fact, he did not know what he thought. New ideas, still inchoate, about behavior, about a man and his woman, crowded together in confusion. He had yet to sort them out. Then,

"I have something to tell you, Sanjak."

"Yes?"

"I shall give you a man child, God willing."

Sanjak felt a sudden sickness, and his hand trembled, causing the shaft to quiver in the sunlight. It was not a sickness that he recognized; it was from a mixture of fear and joy struggling within him for possession of his soul. For all his exploits, he had never fathered a child. He had not replenished the face of the earth for the lives he had sent below. This was not unusual among the Kiowas and Comanches. They were a dying race; their women were not fecund, and few infants who were born survived, with many struck down by measles, smallpox, and other diseases.

Sanjak found Ileeta's hand and held it, looking into her eyes. He was unable to speak. What should he say?

Ileeta intuitively understood his dilemma.

"Your child will be delivered safely; my Lord Jesus tells me so," she said reassuringly.

"Your Medicine?"

"Yes." She fingered the crucifix at her throat.

"But man child or girl, that I cannot promise," she added.

"Whichever it be, let it be. Sanjak will rejoice."

"And your child shall be well cared for—for I know such things as babies need."

Sanjak's fears subsided, but not entirely. During the days and weeks that followed, Sanjak would not leave the vicinity of the lodge except for the most urgent council meetings. Against the winter he strengthened the lodge poles and added buffalo skins to the covering, and new buffalo robes for the couches. Brown Berry and Bird-that-Sings took possession of Ileeta and attended to her every need, indifferent to her protests, regarding the pregnancy as their own, and when from sudden discomfort Ileeta would sigh audibly, they would groan, and Bird-that-Sings would keep up a stream of chatter to amuse or divert her.

While the weather still held and the days were balmy, Sanjak would often go out into the prairie and lie in the sere, tall grass, allowing his anxiety to subside in watching the clouds drift by in the sunlit sky, and gathering reassurance as he contemplated Ileeta's Medicine. Yet his questions continued. What was this Medicine? Above him and around him, he was aware, was the Great Spirit, who governed all things and to whom men might lift their hands and voices in supplication. But the nature of that Spirit was a mystery. With Ileeta it was no mystery; she spoke to a being who was not only Lord of life but also a brother, who understood her voice and spoke to her in her language. She was certain that this being would look after their child.

While lying there, wrapped in his thoughts, a field mouse drawn from its nest by the warmth rustled in the grass nearby and drew Sanjak's attention. His hunter's instinct was aroused; he raised his arm quietly and with a sudden movement had seized the mouse in his hand. For a moment he was on the point of crushing out its life, and then he remembered the incident with the hare. He set the mouse down, rose abruptly, and returned to the lodge. . . .

As the winter deepened, Sanjak spent more time indoors. There was an ample supply of birchwood that made little smoke, and the fire pit in the center of the lodge was kept glowing with coals, the thin smoke drifting upward through the aperture where the lodge poles crossed. Sanjak liked to lie on his side close to Ileeta so he could look at her. She would return his look with eyes that were large and moist and full of wonder, and sometimes she would reach for his hand and lay it on her belly, so that he could feel the leaping within. Then a tender smile would form, and ever so slightly she would draw closer to him, and at these times Sanjak's sickness that was a mingling of fear and joy would return.

Fortunately the winter was mild, and spring followed with a burst of bloom on the redbud, the dogwood in the gullies became a cloud of white, and the fields grew yellow with the coreopsis for which the Kiowas had their own name. Sanjak had to leave to join the spring hunt—from a necessity to replenish the larder—but returned at the earliest to be with Ileeta and to set up the birth lodge. This was a large tepee erected in a grove at some distance from the main camp but not far from Sanjak's lodge.

The camp midwife, old Running Water, superintended the preparations—pits for the fire and for disposal of the after-birth; a soft couch of earth and moss covered with the softest antelope skin with long stakes at the head for the mother to grasp during delivery; a supply of sage and hot coals, rocks to be heated and placed against the back to promote muscle action. The chief medicine man of the band, old Cow-with-a-Hump, who had buffalo power, stood ready if the birth were

61

difficult, and by way of precaution drew a magic line on a buffalo robe and placed it at the door of the lodge. Ileeta, however, needed few of these preparations, but had an easy birth. It began toward dusk one day in early summer.

When Ileeta's labor started, Sanjak returned to his own lodge—it was not allowed for him to be present—and lay stretched on a heap of buffalo robes in a corner, his face to the wall, while at every moan that reached him from the birth lodge he trembled and moaned in response. At the first cry of the newborn, which was like that of pine resin drawn along a bowstring, he stirred weakly, but with gathering strength slowly rose and unsteadily made his way to the other tepee.

Bird-that-Sings now admitted Sanjak to see Ileeta lying on the couch, panting and sweating, but triumph in her eyes, and laughter, and a silent joy in her drawn face.

"It's a male child, your son," announced Bird-that-Sings, when she had washed and wrapped the newborn. "Take it and rejoice."

Sanjak stood for a moment unsteadily; then taking the infant in his arms, he went out of the lodge. Night had fallen. The camp was asleep, and only the barking of a dog and the howl of a distant coyote broke the silence. The night was clear and the sky was full of uncounted stars. Sanjak lifted his son in his arms high above his head and gave a prolonged cry of triumph.

His sickness had passed.

The baby thrived, and with it Sanjak's spirit and vivacity. He took part in the games and the hunts, and now spoke more often in the councils. His speech improved, and his counsel was waited for.

More than these, he liked to be with Ileeta, especially when she was nursing the infant. He had seen much of the world, and he knew how the young of beast and bird were fed, but he had never taken note of a woman nursing her offspring, and he was filled with a kind of awe at the mysterious process of generation and growth—in short, the meaning of motherhood in its totality. As he watched Ileeta bending over the infant and noted the tenderness with which she held him, the authority with which she offered him her breast, the sense of union between the two, the thought came to him that something more than milk passed from mother to son, some ineffable substance, the quality of which eluded him even as he grew the more aware of its existence. Presently Ileeta would look up. Seeing Sanjak, a faint smile would form on her lips, and a light appear in her eyes at once benign with an element of pride and humility mingled.

"Your son," she would whisper. "Does he not grow strong and beautiful—like his father"—not a question, an affirmation.

At times, when she was not nursing or dressing or undressing her son, or preparing his food, or doing other service, or merely playing with his fingers, Ileeta was busy with the duties of the lodge. There were times when the squaws took turns in looking after the infant, for they all considered themselves his mother, or next to his mother, and they equally delighted in him and spent much time playing with him and teaching him to speak.

Ileeta also found time to spend kneeling before her couch, the crucifix held before her, and in this attitude she would murmur words that the others did not understand.

Sanjak observed Ileeta in this posture more than once and supposed that she was talking to her Medicine. What she was saying he did not ask, from respect for her mystery, until one day, as the days grew shorter and coals glowed in the fire pit, sending their smoke and occasional sparks soaring upward through the lodge poles, he said,

"Tell me, does your god—the man on the cross—talk also to you?"

Ileeta smiled.

"He does—in his own way."

Seeing Sanjak's mystification, she went on,

"As a rose speaks."

Sanjak waited.

"I tell you a story. A certain man bought an earthen pot in the market—a pot of red clay such as we have in Mexico. He took it to his house and set it down, and presently a fragrance from the pot filled the room. He spoke to the pot: 'Are you not ordinary clay? From where and how do you give off such fragrance?'

"Then the pot answered and said, 'O foolish man, know you that before I came to you I had been filled with rose petals.'

"If I please you, Sanjak, it is because from childhood I have held Jesus in my heart, from much reading of his words, which I still remember, though I no longer have the book."

Sanjak was silent, while he watched an ember glow and subside, while he contemplated the meaning of Ileeta's parable. Presently she spoke to him.

"It is time we gave our son a name."

"Yes," agreed Sanjak, glad for the diversion. "I have waited until he no longer drank his mother's milk. I have seen many signs, but I must talk to old Cow-with-a-Hump, who will give us the name."

"He may have Kiowa name," assented Ileeta, but added after a moment, in a subdued voice, "but he must be baptized a Christian. I have promised my Jesus—my Medicine. You will say yes?"

Her question was more than a question, a plea for understanding, and she looked at Sanjak with concern in her eyes. There was no Kiowa word for baptism, and she had used the Spanish. Sanjak did not understand. She explained as best she could.

Sanjak knew of the custom among some of the Plains Indians of plunging babies into cold streams—to harden their limbs and spirit, it was said—but this of which Ileeta spoke was a new mystery to him.

Sanjak, fortunately, did not require explanation. The medicine man of the lodge made good medicine and bad, and there was no doubt another kind of good medicine. He was willing for the child to be baptized. When, however, Ileeta said that for baptism they should take their son to a medicine man in the settlement, he protested.

"I will not take you among the settlements," he declared. "You are Mexican, but white, and they will take you away from me."

Ileeta said nothing, and Sanjak saw that she was not happy, and he had a great wish to please her. He also had a great curiosity to know more about this matter of baptism, and indeed about the Medicine Ileeta worshiped.

"But I will take our son," he added, "to find a priest—and return with him safely."

SIX

It was late in a cold afternoon of early winter, on the seventh day of their journey, that Sanjak and his son arrived at the settlement on the edge of the country occupied by the white man. The iron track of the white man, on which cars traveled drawn by a snorting fire engine, entered the town but ended there. Sanjak rode into town slowly, watchful, his son perched before him, both wrapped in blankets against the chill, Sanjak wearing his hair braided and a headband into which a long eagle feather was thrust.

They came to a row of unpainted houses extending on either side of a dusty street, and Sanjak noted the peering faces from half-opened doors as they passed. Farther on the street was filled with traffic—big-wheeled wagons with hooped canvas covers of the kind with which Sanjak was familiar; less familiar vehicles, with high wheels drawn by thin, nervous horses; men on horseback—all making a great cloud of dust such as choked the nostrils of prairie dwellers like Sanjak. There were store buildings with slatted board walkways in front and large glass windows in which could be seen various of the items Peacock offered in trade; people were coming and going on the board walkways with much looking into the windows. But seeing Sanjak, the women would shrink against the wall or hurriedly enter the door.

A man of authority with two short guns strapped to his thighs now stepped into the street before Sanjak and held up his hand.

"Howdy, Charley," he began. "What do you want here?"

Sanjak summoned all his recollection of the English language.

"Me Sanjak, not Charley. Look for priest."

"Very good, Charley—Sanjak," said the man with the guns, and then peering, added, "What's that in your blanket?"

"Papoose," said Sanjak, turning back the coverlet to disclose a face as round and dark as a walnut and two wide-open black eyes gazing at the questioner with questions of their own. "Look for priest—baptize."

"Well, I'll be—" exclaimed the man of authority. He removed a stained hat and scratched his head. "We don't have any priests hereabouts," he said, and then with a look of comprehension, added, "However, we have a man that calls himself a preacher who can do the job. Come with me."

With more courtesy now he led Sanjak to the end of the street and crossed over to the head of the railway track where it ended. Beside it was a red painted building, and on a siding a small red structure on railway wheels. Fastened to the outer wall was a hogshead with a spigot. A short distance away and beside the track was an enclosure in which a herd of cattle milled. The man stopped before the house on wheels and knocked.

A woman came to the door. She had graying hair parted in

the middle and drawn down tightly over her ears into a knot at the back, and she wore spectacles.

"Evening, ma'am," said the man. "Is Ole home?"

"No, marshal, there was a washout up the road apiece, and Ole has his crew mending it. Putting in ballast, I understand. But he should be home shortly. Can I do anything?"

"This here Injun has a papoose he wants baptized. Where he heard about that I don't know, but here he is."

"Well, God be praised for the mystery of his ways." The woman turned to Sanjak.

"What's your name, friend?" she asked.

"Sanjak. Kiowa of the Nut Eater band."

"Well, won't you get down and come in? Mr. Svenson will be in shortly and will take care of you. Thank you, marshal." The marshal left.

"Sanjak wait here," said Sanjak, unwilling to enter the house.

"Then let me see your—son or daughter—?"

"Boy papoose."

"Your son!" Drawing a shawl around her shoulders, she came down the steps to the pony's side and peered at the child. "My," she exclaimed admiringly, "what a handsome boy," and from her voice and smile Sanjak knew that she liked his son. He was pleased with her; she was different from Ileeta, she made him think of Ileeta—the way Ileeta had clung to the baby before handing him up to Sanjak, and the look in her eyes as she had held Sanjak's hand, unwilling to let him go. "My Lord Jesus will protect you," Ileeta had whispered and then impulsively had brought his hand to her lips and kissed it.

"But he must be hungry," Mrs. Svenson was saying. "Let me bring him in, and I'll put some porridge on."

"Him not hungry. Eat pemmican. Very good."

"Really?" commented Mrs. Svenson. "But he must be tired. Have you come from far?"

Sanjak, for answer, held up his hands with three fingers depressed.

"Him go sleep mighty quick," he agreed.

"Then let me take him and put him to rest," urged Mrs. Svenson.

Sanjak allowed the woman to take his son in her arms, and again he noticed her way of handling him, so like Ileeta's.

"My, what a fine boy," Mrs. Svenson repeated as she cooed to the child, who stared up at her questioningly but without protest. "He seems mighty clean for such a long journey," she commented.

"Sanjak know how to keep papoose clean," said Sanjak with pride. "Ileeta show."

"Ileeta. Who's Ileeta?"

"Papoose mama."

"Well, if you won't come in, you just make yourself comfortable until Ole returns. Meanwhile, I'm getting supper ready and will see to it your little one gets rested."

Sanjak dismounted and hobbled his pony, which went to nibbling the dry grass around the house.

Ole Svenson was late in returning, and lamplight glowed through the little window of the house on wheels to mingle its light with that of the rising moon, illuminating Sanjak sitting taciturn and meditative on the steps leading to the door. There was a metallic clangor in the distance, and a strange vehicle that rode on the rails loomed, with several men standing on it and working a bar up and down. It halted at a little distance, and all the men but one went off to another red house set beside the tracks, while one approached. He was tall and gaunt, taller far than Sanjak, and he came slowly, from a great weariness. For some reason Sanjak's eyes dimmed, so that the man appeared to swim toward him, a vast presence congealing from a fog, as a mother's breast must seem to the infant hungering for nourishment—Sanjak only knew that the presence was friendly, yea, more than friendly, a haven, a welcome, with an encompassing compassion.

The imagery and the sensation dissolved; Ole Svenson was standing before Sanjak, a man with a pale face, very begrimed, thin yellow hair that hung in damp strands below his ears, and eyes that were very blue, like the blue of the sky, and he was speaking, in a very matter-of-fact way,

"Good day, friend. You have been waiting for me?"

"You priest?" asked Sanjak. Mr. Svenson did not look like a priest, at least the priests that Sanjak had seen in Mexico, who wore long skirts like women.

"I am not a priest, but I am ordained and authorized to administer the sacraments," Svenson replied in a voice that lilted, quite different from the gutturals of the Kiowa, so that Sanjak had to strain his attention. He understood neither the words nor Svenson's way of using them, but he sensed that Svenson understood his need.

At that moment Mrs. Svenson opened the door.

"Ole dear," she explained, "this young man has brought a baby to be baptized."

"A baby?" said Svenson in some surprise. "That is a good work for the Lord. Go in, friend, and let us thank God.

"But first," he recollected himself, "we must refresh you. You have traveled far?"

Taking a dipper from a nail in the wall, he drew water from the hogshead and offered Sanjak a drink. Sanjak was not thirsty, but took this as a sign of hospitality, much as he would have if offered a pipe, and drank. He returned the dipper to Mr. Svenson, who drank deeply and refilled the dipper and drank again with the thirst of a man who was exhausted. Svenson now filled a hand basin and, setting it on a bench, offered it to Sanjak. Sanjak washed his face and dried it on a towel Svenson handed him, and then emptied the pan. Svenson washed his face, using a great deal of soap, and when he finished, much of his weariness had passed and the pale skin of his face glowed with a pinkish translucence.

"Now, we go in and sup," he said.

Sanjak entered the box car and found himself in a square chamber half as large as his lodge, partitioned in the middle. The front room was fitted with a stove and cupboard, a table and some chairs, curtained at the windows, and some pictures on the wall. One of these was of the man Jesus, except that he was not on a cross but was in a field and held in his arms a small animal. Sanjak recognized it from his raids into Mexico; it was a lamb, the young of a fleece-covered animal called sheep.

"You friend," said Sanjak happily. "We smoke peace pipe together."

Mr. Svenson smiled. "I don't smoke, but we will break bread together, which is the same."

Fortunately for Sanjak, supper consisted of a stew, which did not require the use of the white man's tools except a spoon, and Sanjak was familiar with that. He knew coffee, which was supplied the Indians by the traders, but he liked this better than what Bird-that-Sings prepared.

During the meal Mr. Svenson explained his occupation as that of a "section boss" supervising a crew that maintained the railroad tracks, and the cause of his delay and weariness. A winter cloudburst up the road several miles had washed away the ballast and spread the rails, causing a derailment of a locomotive and some cars in which several trespassing riders were injured and one killed. The train had been righted and put back on the tracks, and the dead man removed, and it was now the job of Svenson and his crew to repair the track in time for the resumption of traffic.

After supper Mr. Svenson drew the lamp nearer, and taking a book from the shelf, opened it.

"Now we read. We always read the Good Book after supper," he explained in his high and lilting voice that seemed to Sanjak now very melodious, like an Indian crooning. "I trust you will agree, and then we will talk about your son."

"Sanjak listen," said Sanjak. "Don't know English good."

"We will make it short tonight."

He opened the book and read,

"He that entereth in by the door is the shepherd of the sheep. . . ."

There was more that Sanjak did not understand, but he remembered the end, for he subsequently spent much time thinking of it.

"I am the good shepherd: the good shepherd giveth his life for the sheep."

It was an allegory he understood. Sheep, of course, were unfamiliar to him; but he knew horses, and in Mexico he had seen Mexican shepherds grazing their sheep on the hillsides and leading them back to the sheepfolds in the village, and what Mr. Svenson was reading, together with the picture on the wall, evoked memories of his raiding forays into Mexico.

Mr. Svenson had finished reading.

"Now, as to baptizing your son. Why do you wish him baptized?"

"His mama Christian. Mexican woman. Say to baptize and make him Christian."

"You wish it also?" asked Mr. Svenson.

"What Ileeta wish, Sanjak wish."

Mr. Svenson meditated on this, his deep-set and pale blue eyes bent on his guest.

"Do you wish to know what baptism means?"

"Yes, talk."

Mr. Svenson undertook to explain. He did better than Ileeta, but most of what he said went over Sanjak's head. He spoke of sin, as something that offended the man Jesus—something Sanjak faintly understood, for the Great Spirit and all the lesser spirits must be propitiated, and their taboos respected; but the idea of forgiveness of which Mr. Svenson spoke escaped him, and the meaning of Jesus dying on a cross—of the shepherd giving his life for his sheep—these were matters beyond his present comprehension.

Finally, Mr. Svenson said, "Your son is still an infant. Before I baptize him, you must undertake, as father, to rear him in the Christian faith. Do you so promise?"

When the question had been put several ways, Sanjak finally understood and nodded vigorously.

"Since there are no Christians in your lodge besides your wife, you must agree to bring him to a Christian school as soon as he is old enough to learn. Do you promise?"

Again the nod and a grunt.

Mrs. Svenson had earlier fed the baby some porridge, and he was now sleeping soundly. He responded without a murmur, however, beyond a small whimper when Mrs. Svenson took him up and handed him to Sanjak. Mr. Svenson now took the child in his arms.

"What name do I give this child?"

"I call him *Pee-a-koo*, which mean Spotted Horse. Ileeta say to name him after Christian man Pedro."

"Good, that is Peter in English." Mr. Svenson dipped his fingers in a bowl of water and laid his hand gently on the baby's head. "Spotted Horse Peter, I baptize thee in name of Father, Son, and Holy Ghost. Amen."

Spotted Horse Peter, who had until now been very quiet, eyeing the proceedings with wide-eyed wonder, shuddered and whimpered.

Mr. Svenson now bent his head and kissed the baby on the forehead, and when he looked at Sanjak his eyes were moist.

"You have a fine boy," he said softly. "Watch after him well."

Svenson was silent for a moment; his pale blue eyes rested on Sanjak in a kind of transport.

"Maybe, one day you will be a Christian, no?" he said fervently, with a coaxing urgency. "When the Lord Jesus comes into your heart, you will be a changed man. You will love everybody, you will want everybody to be happy. You won't want to hurt anybody."

Svenson did not press the point.

"But now," he said, "it is late. You will stay the night. We can stable your pony at the horse corral, where he can get a feed of oats." He turned to his wife. "Christina, will you again look after our young one while our guest and I tend to his pony?"

They stepped out of the house into a change of weather. It had grown colder, and the sky was heavily overcast. By the time they had found the pony, which with its hobbles had not strayed far, and had properly stabled it, even Sanjak was ready to return to the warmth of the little house and to sit in the strange chair by the side of the potbellied stove. Svenson sat in another that had half hoops on the bottom, and as he talked in his lilting way he would go back and forth and up and down in his chair, as though in cadence with his voice. He did not talk much about himself, but he showed a great interest in his guest—about Sanjak's tribe, his family, their customs.

Sanjak was greatly impressed by Mr. Svenson, as he had been by his wife, and thought the Christians were good people. He should know more about them.

SEVEN

During the night the wind rose to a howl and shook the railway shack as it tore at the roof and siding. Snow began to fall and fell all the next day. It was characteristic of the Indians to remain close in during snow or storm, and in any case it was no weather to travel with an infant in arms. When the Svensons insisted that Sanjak must remain with them until the storm abated, he was content to stay. Eager as he was to return to his lodge, he was also held by a certain curiosity to know about white men like the Svensons. Apart from trips to the stable by Sanjak to care for the pony, and by Svenson to the workmen's quarters to see to their needs, they remained indoors. Mr. Svenson spent much of his time reading from his Bible, while Mrs. Svenson mended clothing and did other household tasks, and attended to Spotted Horse Peter under Sanjak's watchful eye.

Svenson did not intrude upon Sanjak's thoughts, except that from time to time he would start a short conversation in which he told about his early years in Sweden, his migration to America, and his finding work in the new railway construction. Svenson was past the age of military service but he had two sons, he said, who were in the army.

"Soon, we hope, the war will be over," he commented. There had been a big battle during the preceding summer at a place called Gettysburg, in which the Northern armies had turned back the Southern offensive, and during the same days the armies of General Grant had captured Vicksburg on the Great River. It would be only a matter of time, Svenson thought, before the white men were at peace and united, and the building of the railway westward would proceed. The ominous import of these developments for the Indians seemed to escape Svenson, but it left Sanjak uneasy. If the white men could all be like Svenson, he thought, there could be peace with the Indians. The white men had much to teach the Indians, not only in skills but in ideas of behavior.

The storm continued for another day, and then the skies cleared and the sun shone, and it was necessary to get the work crew out clearing the drifted snow from the railway tracks and strengthening the rails so trains could move. Travel on horse with an infant in this weather and these conditions would still be hazardous, however, and Sanjak offered to help Svenson. Svenson was pleased, for he was short-handed, but he hesitated.

"This is not your kind of work," he said.

Sanjak threw out his arms.

"Sanjak will learn. Sanjak learn quick," he said confidently. "Have strong arms."

Sanjak spent the day with the men and, under Svenson's supervision, learned how to hold and use a shovel, a pick, a crowbar, how to drive a spike and how to loosen one—all of which information lodged in his mind to be retrieved at a later date under tragic circumstances.

The men on the crew were a strange mixture of unfamiliar races, many of them speaking English little better than Sanjak. They were men of broad shoulders and heavy sinews, with a capacity for hard work far beyond that of Sanjak, who discovered his back aching from the lifting and his palms growing raw from the tool handles. Unlike most of the white men whom Sanjak had encountered, they were of docile, almost timid disposition, as though they had been in slavery. Svenson was gentle with them; he had a way of coaxing the greatest efforts from them while showing them the utmost consideration. Sanjak was impressed again with a quality in the man, which, he thought, must derive from his Christian god.

The men were, it was explained to Sanjak, newly come to the Great Plains; they had been born and reared in lands across the Great Waters—a distance impossible for him to imagine who had never seen the sea. They had come to establish homes in this new land and were now working to obtain means to pay the passage for their families left behind. Sanjak understood. Many of the tribal braves, before they acquired squaws, would often be gone as long as two years on their raids into Mexico and elsewhere. Still, it was a trying experience to be separated from one's tribe and community for so long, and a feeling akin to sympathy went out to them. He had few words with them, nor had they much to say to him, but they did not regard him—to them a savage—with unfriendliness. Sanjak appreciated that; he liked people.

Sanjak spent three days working with the men, learning each day new skills in handling the white man's tools and in working metal. By then the weather had abated, the tracks were again passable, and he prepared to leave.

It was now Sunday when work ceased on the railway, and Svenson suggested to Sanjak that he might like to attend church with them before setting out.

"You pray to your god for safe journey for Sanjak?" Sanjak asked.

"Yes."

"Then I go to church."

Bundling up Spotted Horse Peter in his blankets, the four of them set out. A path had been cleared on the board sidewalk to the church, which was a white painted structure at the end of the main street, marked by a spired steeple. Already people were gathering for the services, and along a hitching rail were farm wagons, surreys, and other vehicles, the horses covered with blankets against the cold. In the interior of the building were probably two score persons, farm families sitting together on long benches, men, women, and children. At one end was a raised platform enclosed by a railing, and a tall box on which rested a large book. The congregation looked enquiringly at Sanjak and his burden, but smiled to him in a friendly way and made room for him and Mrs. Svenson on one of the benches. Mr. Svenson mounted the platform and announced a hymn.

There was much singing. After a song Svenson would call out:

"Let us now try number seventeen. Now, all together."

And his face lighted, and to Sanjak it appeared to shine, and his blue eyes held a new radiance as he lifted his voice. It wasn't music to which Sanjak was used, but it was not unpleasant, except for the man beside Svenson who made sounds that hurt his ears from what was called a fiddle.

After a while Svenson began to speak to the people. Sanjak could not follow what he said; there were words that confused him—"washed in the blood," "rebirth," "sacrifice of the cross," and "Lamb of God," and others.

At the close of his talk there was another hymn during which Svenson invited those who wished "to accept the Lord Jesus as Savior" to come to the rail. Sanjak did not understand this, but the hymn, first read by Svenson, was sung repeatedly until it remained very clear in Sanjak's memory and gave him much to ponder. It went:

Just as I am, without one plea,
But that thy blood was shed for me,
And that thou bid'st me come to thee,
O Lamb of God, I come! I come!

As the singing continued, Svenson looked hopefully over the room for someone to come forward, and more than once Sanjak felt Svenson's invoking eyes on him. Presently, a girl not yet ready for childbearing, a shawl about her shoulders and on her head a bonnet that concealed her face, came forward timidly and knelt with downcast head.

"God bless you, my child," said Svenson, placing his hand gently upon her shoulder, and then straightening, looked over his congregation and enquired in a gentle, pleading tone,

"Will another join this newborn child of God?"

But no one else came forward, and after a while Svenson announced a "Communion." This, Sanjak noted, was a ceremony in which almost everyone went to the railing and knelt while Svenson gave to each a morsel of bread followed by a sip from a stemmed cup, at the same time speaking softly some words the meaning of which Sanjak could not grasp.

After the services there was much talking and handshaking among the people, and several came to speak to Mrs. Svenson, who introduced Sanjak as "our new brother, Mr. Sanjak, of the Kiowa people." Some of the children, however, hung back or hid behind their mothers' skirts while they peeked around furtively at Sanjak.

On returning to their lodgings, passing through the streets of the settlement and across the strip of raw prairie to where the railroad tracks ran, Mrs. Svenson commented on the service.

"You gave a powerful sermon, Ole," she assured her husband. "It was the Lord's triumph to bring the Tazey girl to the rail—a sweet thing—and now we'll pray that the rest of her family may be led to follow her."

"It would be the Lord's work," commented Svenson with a

certain sadness in his voice, "if he would touch some of the men in my work crew."

"Just be patient, Ole," consoled his wife, "and wait upon the Lord, and in his time he will gather them in, and you will see them kneeling at the rail."

"O what a joy to serve the Lord," she continued in repressed enthusiasm as they neared the tracks. "What a change you will experience, Mr. Sanjak, when the Spirit of the Lord touches you with his grace."

Sanjak accepted this silently. It was all mysterious to him, but he was glad he had come.

EIGHT

The weather had rapidly cleared, and Sanjak's return to the tribe was without incident. He was a good provider and nurse to his son, feeding him with pemmican and corn meal cakes Ileeta had prepared for the journey. He talked with his son endlessly, to which the child, held in front of him, responded with gurgles and babbling, and snatches of intelligible speech.

As he traveled south and west, he found less snow, until it was but a thin crust through which the grass rose tall and sparkling and crackled under the pony's hooves. Within a week they were again in sight of the lodges. He recognized his own tepee and saw the smoke curling above the crossed poles.

THE KIOWA

When he was within bowshot of his lodge, Sanjak let out his Kiowa cry of the returning warrior, expecting Ileeta to appear at the tepee opening.

When none of his squaws appeared, he forced his pony to a gallop, and at the lodge slid off with his burden, tossed the halter strap to one of the Indian boys playing about, and hurried within.

Ileeta was lying against the tepee wall. Her eyes turned toward him, and they were dark and ominous.

"I have brought our son home safely," cried Sanjak. "He is now a Christian."

Ileeta only continued to stare at him.

"Are you sick?" asked Sanjak.

Ileeta did not answer.

Sanjak was puzzled. Had Brown Berry or Bird-that-Sings so failed to answer him, he would have reproached them with some bit of sardonic humor, but with Ileeta he had great patience.

"Would you see our son?" he asked. "He is well and strong. Look."

Ileeta held out her arms, and Sanjak came and placed the baby in them. She clutched the child and held him to her tightly, bent over him and smothered him with kisses. Then with a convulsive shudder she turned away and, holding the baby, faced the tepee wall. Her slender body continued to quiver, and muffled sobs filled the lodge.

Sanjak's puzzlement grew.

"Why does she behave thus?" asked Sanjak of Brown Berry, who was standing by.

Brown Berry, unwilling to reply, looked away.

At this Sanjak's wrath began to mount.

"Tell me," he demanded, his voice growing strident, "what is the matter." Brown Berry began to whimper.

"He—he—forced Ileeta."

"Forced—who—?"

"He—he seized Ileeta while she washed by the river. Ileeta now is sick."

The marriage bonds among the Kiowas and Comanches were both tight and loose. Squaws were known to desert their husbands for another who better pleased their fancy, at no more cost sometimes than the levy of a pony by the tribal council upon the acquiring male. But to take an unwilling woman was another matter. That the taking of Ileeta was by force Sanjak had no doubt.

"He—who is this man?" he shouted, and laid hand on the hatchet in his belt. When Sanjak's wrath was aroused, it was as though the sky darkened.

There was a silence, and then the name burst forth.

"Running Wolf."

"Ah," he said in a whisper. "Running Wolf." And his hatred of the man rose uncontrollably. Bowing his head, he began to chant, half-heard, a Kiowa song of avengement, but woven with words and expressions of his own:

> *Red neck bird in robe of black:*
> *Wait on yonder treetop;*
> *Wait—but wait,*
> *And you may change your dress of black*
> *To one of red—of sunset red,*
> *While you thrust your head*
> *Into the entrails of my enemy.*

And added in a whisper, "for I shall kill Running Wolf."

Though spoken in a whisper, the words did not escape Ileeta, who now turned suddenly.

"Oh, no, you must not. No, no, no."

Sanjak raised his head and regarded Ileeta with glazed eyes, in which there might have been a trace of the sardonic.

"You don't want Running Wolf punished?" he asked.

"No."

"This is strange. Is this so common then among the Mexican women?" he asked, bitterness creeping into his voice.

"It is not the first time."

Sanjak's eyes grew hot with fire. He had never known

jealousy, had never had occasion to; but now something akin to jealousy rose within him. It was unjustified, if he gave it thought, and afterward he would regret it, but at the moment his soul was shaken at the prospect that Ileeta was not entirely his.

"Running Wolf?"

"No—in Mexico. As I told you, I belonged to no one and had no one to protect me—as you have done."

Ileeta was weeping, and her tears now affected Sanjak.

"Is that reason to allow another . . .?"

"We must forgive. Promise me you will not harm Running Wolf. What happened to me is not important, but if you start a blood feud with Running Wolf, where will it end? Running Wolf's family will then avenge themselves on you. No, you must forgive."

Sanjak had to think about this. Running Wolf's only near male relative was a boy, Howling Dog, son of Running Wolf's sister. He sat, and while he sat his anger abated.

"Is this what your Jesus says?" he asked presently.

It was hardly necessary to ask, for Svenson had repeated the idea several times during his week with the track foreman.

"Yes," said Ileeta emphatically. "My Lord says we must forgive those who do evil to us."

Sanjak was again silent. Presently he said, "I must think about this."

He went out into the evening. Dusk had fallen, and stars were already beginning to appear. Sanjak's gaze roved the skies as though to find somewhere the spirit of the Jesus whom Ileeta worshiped, and who at times seemed to be an invisible presence by her side, hoping that perhaps from him he might gain wisdom to understand the woman Ileeta and the will to abide by her wishes.

After a while he reentered the tepee. "I will not kill Running Wolf," he said, but conviction was not in his voice.

Ileeta was holding her child, and now Sanjak's words caused her face to lighten with peace, but Sanjak's heart was heavy. This kind of conduct he did not understand, and there was, besides, the matter of his honor among the tribe, a thing he did understand. Nevertheless, as the days passed he was able to conceal his wrath and bitterness, and with such success that Running Wolf thought Ileeta had been shrewd and had told no one of his adventure with her.

NINE

Running Wolf had a malady, a distemper that did not trouble him, but communicated itself to Ileeta and produced a suppuration that did not heal, so that she did not permit Sanjak to approach her. At the same time her mood darkened, and she began to waste away. The passing of winter, the warmth of spring, when the redbud flowered and the prairie scintillated in variegated color, brought no relief, and the coming of summer only aggravated the malady.

Ileeta began an intermittent bleeding that could not be stanched. Bird-that-Sings gave such aid and comfort as she could, without effect, and then Sanjak's mother, the squaw Sweet Grass, breaking a tribal taboo, visited her son's lodge to minister with such unguents and herbal preparations as her older wisdom taught were therapeutic. Finally, old Cow-with-a-Hump, the man of great medicine, was called in, who made incantations and held over her his parfleche bag of mystery. Ileeta continued to sicken.

"The white men have powerful medicine," Sanjak declared. "I will go to Svenson."

Before he could leave, however, the great rains of autumn had begun. The band had moved south from the high prairie to a grove in the bottoms of the Cimmaron more protected from the cold north winds. The rain, however, became a deluge without equal in the memory of the oldest man. The ground grew soft, and a new flooring of buffalo hides had to be spread, and the ditches around the lodge were deepened to drain away the water.

The rain continued without let, accompanied by sudden gusts of wind that shook the lodge poles and sent a howling among the trees of the grove. The small store of dried wood and stems kept for the fire had been used up, and now despite the dew cloth, or inner lining of buffalo skins, the rain began to come through the roof aperture. It dampened the small fire of buffalo chips and caused the lodge to fill with acrid smoke that set the occupants to coughing.

From time to time, as the five huddled against the lodge walls to keep dry, they were illuminated by flashes of lightning—Bird-that-Sings's face drawn in terror, Brown Berry huddling with head bent over Spotted Horse Peter, whom she held in her arms—his large dark eyes filled with a wonderful curiosity at this interesting world into which he had been introduced—Sanjak stonily impassive, Ileeta with weary and pain-filled eyes regarding her lord with a distress of compassion.

Suddenly the lodge was filled with blue light, followed immediately by a clap of thunder that deafened the ears, this in turn by a great crashing of timber at the very door of the lodge, it seemed, that caused even Sanjak to start.

"*Ei, ei, ei,*" keened Bird-that-Sings in uncontrollable fright. "The sky dogs are upon us. *Ei, ei, ei.*"

Ileeta had felt for Sanjak's hand and was holding it tight. Now she released it as he rose and went to the lodge door. An ancient and mighty elm had been riven by a bolt, sending a great spar hurtling among the lesser growth and barely missing the lodge. Sanjak seized his hatchet and his buffalo robe, dashed to the fallen tree, and holding the robe as a shelter, began to hack off pieces of the dry core of the fallen timber. With these he renewed the lodge fire until he had filled a pot with coals; these he brought and set beside Ileeta to warm her.

She smiled wanly at him, and whispered,

"You are good to me, Sanjak."

The rain fell off, but the water began to rise in the river and to overflow the banks. Old Cow-with-a-Hump, the wise one of the Nut Eaters, consulted his medicine and announced that the band would move to the higher ground of the prairie.

It did not take long to set the band in movement, but with the water-soaked skins and the soggy ground the work was hard. Brown Berry returned Spotted Horse Peter to the arms of his mother and drew a buffalo robe over them to protect them from the rain. With Sanjak's aid and direction the squaws stowed all the lodge furnishings in their rawhide bags, then dismantled the lodge, carefully wrapping the lodge skins wet side out and binding them to a travois made of the lodge poles. Sanjak now carried out Ileeta and Spotted Horse Peter in their covering and laid them on another travois while the squaws loosed the tethered ponies.

The entire band was in movement. Sanjak, hurrying ahead, found a piece of thick turf on an elevation and directed the erection of the lodge there. The rain, however, continued to fall, whipped into gusts by the stronger winds of the uplands, and the occupants of the lodge could do little but shiver in their damp garments. The day ended and the night, but the rain continued without let.

Ileeta's illness was aggravated by the weather; her face grew hot as her body shivered with chill, and she began to cough spasmodically, with flecks of blood in her spittle. Sanjak grew alarmed.

"I go to the settlements," he announced to Ileeta. "I fetch white men who can make you well."

Ileeta turned to him with a wan look.

"You are good to me, Sanjak," she said again. "Stay with me. The settlement is too far; it will take too long to go and to come again. I will not be here when you return."

Sanjak meditated on this while the rain beat on the walls and in fine mist drifted through the lodge. Death—Sanjak had witnessed it in his thirty years—in the raids, in the hunt, in the camp—but not in his own lodge. It had not occurred to him that in dying Ileeta would be taken from him, never to be near again. As earlier he had been brought face to face through Ileeta with the phenomenon of birth and motherhood, so now through her he was confronted by the phenomena of love and death, union and separation. It was beyond his comprehension. He was not prepared for separation from Ileeta; yet now the prospect stood before him in all its palpable reality—like an advancing fog, enclosing and suffocating him.

Divining his confusion, his trauma, Ileeta reached out for his hand.

"Be not sad, Sanjak. If I go, it is only for a time. Then we shall be together again—forever."

"Forever? I do not know forever. So long as the sun shines and grass grows? How?"

"Longer. When the sun is darkened and the earth is cold, we shall remain together. My Jesus tells me so. Be not sad. . . . Yet I am sad that I must go now, before our son is grown. Care for him, Sanjak. Teach him your arts and skills but also to be a Christian."

The speech was too much for her. She lay back on the couch and closed her eyes. Sanjak still held her hand, while the rain continued to beat on the lodge wall and the rush of the wind caused the poles to tremble.

Against the opposite wall Brown Berry crouched under a buffalo robe to keep dry, and now she began to cry with little spasmodic whimpers.

THE KIOWA

"Hush," said Sanjak quietly, but Brown Berry continued to whimper, while outside the rain continued its steady threnody.

TEN

The Kiowas, before coming down from the mountains in the time of the forefathers, had buried their dead with the knees bent upon the chest, the head drawn forward, and the body lashed in this position while still warm. After confederating with the Comanches and other Plains Indians, they had followed the custom of leaving the dead on a scaffold, or in a tree, to protect the corpse from predatory animals. In such cases the form was left full-length, with hands to the sides.

Sanjak rejected both customs in the case of Ileeta. "She was a Christian," he told Brown Berry and Bird-that-Sings. "She would not want it this way."

He had the women lay her carefully on a travois, full-length, with her hands crossed upon her breast, holding her crucifix, and then wrapped and bound, as a papoose is bound on a cradleboard.

At the last moment, however, before the binding, he removed the crucifix and placed it about his own neck.

Then he mounted the pony that drew the travois. The rain had ceased. The sky was clear, the day filled with lambent light.

Brown Berry and Bird-that-Sings had been moaning as they went about their task, but now they burst into loud wailing.

Sanjak cowed them with the fierceness of his looks.

"There must be no wailing—and no cutting of yourselves with knives and flint," he commanded. "It is not the Christian way. Do you understand?"

The women were submissive. Putting the baby in their care, Sanjak rode out into the prairie.

He traveled that day and the following day, and another night and a day, stopping only to rest the pony, until he came to the foothills of the Wichita uplift. Here he climbed among the granite boulders until he found a narrow recess, a shallow cave with an earthen floor, of which he had known from hunting, and here, after digging a grave with his war ax and hunting knife, he buried Ileeta.

He covered her body with earth and gravel and then rolled stones upon it in a little mound, and then went about to find *bois d'arc*, the prairie wood that does not rot, to fashion therewith a cross as a head mark. But after a little while he left off, threw the marker away, and smoothed the carpet of stones.

"Her Jesus knows where to find her—and so do I," he considered to himself. "It is enough."

For a week longer, until the old moon had waned and the new moon showed, Sanjak remained in the hills near the grave, fasting but for a little pemmican from his bag and a little water from the spring, making no sound, except that when the moon would appear on the ridge, for whose coming he would lie awake, he would begin to moan softly, as a drowsing dog does, and continue for a space until exhausted, and then drawing his blanket about him against the cold, he would fall asleep.

He was not yet ready to return to his lodge. Instead he rode west into the high prairies where there were no trees but only the sere grass on a vast tableland that lay very close to the sky. He came to a camp of the Kwahadi Comanches, whose chief was the noted raider Buzzard Quill. The Comanches were hospitable but left him to his brooding, and he remained with them until winter came on; then he left them and headed his pony east.

He traveled slowly, unable to face returning to his lodge in which Ileeta was no longer there to welcome him. Snow was falling when the camp dogs announced his arrival to his two squaws. They received him without question or without curiosity, respecting his reticence, treating him as one who had been on a hunt or foray, set food before him and gave him fresh breechclout and shirt.

After some days of sitting in his lodge while Brown Berry and Bird-that-Sings went about their work, he resumed meeting with the Red Leg Society at their smoke lodge. But he was a taciturn member, seldom raising his voice in council, in which the talk was mainly about the increase in the white man's slaughter of the buffalo and the more frequent presence of horse soldiers crossing the tribal lands. Several times in the following days he caught sight of Running Wolf, who was not a member of the Red Leg Society, and who somehow managed to lodge in other parts of the camp or avoid meeting up with Sanjak. Sanjak's hatred smoldered and could not be quenched.

ELEVEN

The year passed and the time for the fall hunt came, but game was scarce and the pursuit of the buffalo moved in small parties toward the high plains, where the white hunters with the long guns were still few in number. Here the grass was short and sparse and gave way to vast stretches of gaunt and empty earth cut by deep gullies and inhabited only by the prairie rodents that lived in underground cells.

Sanjak had ridden out alone from the camp, searching for some glen where either buffalo or antelope might be found grazing, and it was there that he came upon a wolf feeding upon one of the prairie rodents he had caught. The hunter's instinct in Sanjak rose to the challenge and mingled with the smoldering resentments that ranged for release in combat. He quietly approached from downwind and was not twenty paces away when the wolf sniffed his presence and turned to face him, growling.

Sanjak nudged his mount, and the pony leaped forward.

For a moment the wolf stood its ground, teeth bared, and snarled, not daring to attack but retreating as Sanjak charged. Then the animal turned tail and ran.

Sanjak pursued. The wolf was fast and for a few minutes outran the palomino, weighted as he was with a rider. But presently the pony gained. The wolf changed direction and back, but the pony was a well-trained hunter and turned almost as quickly. Soon man and rider gained upon their game and were racing alongside.

Then Sanjak gave a flying leap and caught the wolf by the throat. For a moment there was a violent struggle, with wolf claws tearing at Sanjak's leather shirt, but the Indian's powerful hands continued to squeeze the animal's throat, never relenting for a second, and presently it grew quiet.

Then, swiftly reaching with one hand for the thongs at his waist, Sanjak bound the wolf's jaws shut and deftly trussed the legs. Releasing his grip on the animal's throat, he allowed it to breathe. There was a renewed threshing and muffled snarling, but without effect. The wolf was captive to the Indian.

Chanting the song of the successful hunter, Sanjak started toward the camp. The chase, the struggle, the victory had elated him, had washed away for the time his moroseness, his sad remembrances, the bitterness of his mood. The sun was lowering in the west, throwing a sheen upon the reddish earth of the flats and casting long shadows where the boulders lay upon the surface. A raw wind had risen, but Sanjak did not notice; he rather liked to listen to its rustling in the desert bush and in the grass.

There was another sound in the wind. Sanjak was instantly alert. It was faint and distant. Sanjak scanned the horizon, and turned his pony against the wind so that, like a white man's weathervane, he could catch the direction of the sound.

Not far away the earth was lifted in a low and gravelly ridge, and as Sanjak rode in that direction the cry became more distinct, still faint—but recognizably human.

Suddenly before him gaped a fault in the earth, a narrow crevice wrought not by erosion but by some subterranean movement, not fathomless, but deep, and narrow with precipitous walls.

Sanjak dropped from his pony and peered down in the dusk. He could not see; yet he recognized the voice.

"Ah, Running Wolf," he exclaimed. "What are you doing down there?"

"Sanjak!" cried the other with a rasping voice that was both joyful and uneasy. "It's Sanjak."

"Yes, it's Sanjak. And what are you doing down there?"

"I fell. I tried to leap the ditch, but my pony balked. I was thrown off and here I am. I think I have broken a bone. Help me out."

"I must think about that," responded Sanjak. "I cannot see well into the pit. How far down are you?"

"It must be the height of three men."

"Can you not climb?"

"The walls are smooth. I have no place to put hands or feet."

"Are you comfortable?"

"I am hungry—and thirsty. Have you nothing you can let down?"

"Ah, yes," answered Sanjak reflectively. "But is there no way out except above?"

"None, Sanjak. Now throw me down a cord that I may climb out."

"I have none so long, and the camp is at a distance."

"Then send me some food, Sanjak, for I am hungry. I have eaten nothing for two days."

"Two days, that's not long. On the raids we often ate nothing for two days. There was the raid to Mexico where I—I mean you—found Ileeta. Do you remember?"

"Yes, yes, Sanjak. But now I am hungry."

Sanjak was suddenly silent. Presently, "Sanjak, Sanjak. Are you there?" The voice was pitiful, pleading.

"Yes, I am here. I am thinking."

"You always think."

"Yes, I know. Now I am thinking what I can do for you."

Thoughts—dark thoughts—and more than thoughts, dark passions, violent passions, passions born of bitter grievance and cruel injustice agitated his spirit, lashed out as with a whip, and drove away instincts of tribal solidarity, all bonds of racial brotherhood, all nascent compassion and budding forgiveness nurtured by the spell and memory of the Mexican woman. In their stead the means of vengeance rose before him, retribution in accord with tribal justice; it possessed his spirit, ravished him with a vision of sadistic satisfaction.

From below came Running Wolf's voice, now querulous and complaining and insistent.

"You think too much. You must do something. I am thirsty."

Running Wolf's plea, rather than softening, hardened Sanjak's lust; contempt for weakness added to hatred.

"Yes, I have thought of something," he now announced. "I am sending you company, one to give you milk and meat."

"Ah, that is good. That is very good. For I am very hungry."

Sanjak returned to his pony, where the wolf lay gagged and bound to the surcingle. He hesitated for a moment, then loosening the animal, he carried it to the edge of the pit. He slit the thongs that bound the legs and the lashings of the jaws, and held the animal poised over the lip of the crevice.

"Here," he called down into the gloom, "is your mistress, at whose teats you may suck milk, and with whom you may lie to keep you warm."

And he thrust the wolf into the pit. From below in an instant issued screams, snarls, growls, and moans.

But by the time the screams had receded to moans and had died away, Sanjak was far distant and out of hearing.

When, next afternoon, Sanjak returned to the band and found his lodge, he was met by Bird-that-Sings, who immediately began to cry over his torn shirt and the caked blood upon his chest.

"You have fallen upon misfortune," she wailed. "What has befallen you?"

"I fell among thorns," responded Sanjak, an explanation that to Bird-that-Sings was obviously inadequate. But when she began to protest and to wheedle for more information, he bade her shortly to be silent and to say nothing of his condition.

PART

3

The
White
Man's
Road

ONE

When members of the band found Running Wolf's mangled body, some questioned how the wolf had fallen into the same pit—or whether it had fallen at all, a thing unbelievable. But none raised the question with Sanjak. Still, it was known that Sanjak had ridden in from the same region the day before, that his shirt was torn, his chest clawed and bleeding, and there were shrewd ones who had their suspicions. And most of all, his cause for vengeance—a cause that had never been requited—was well known.

Then again, it may have been Sanjak's imagination, reading into curious and silent glances thoughts that were not there, finding a hidden cause when this or that brave seemed to avoid him or failed to salute him from a distance.

More deeply troubling him was the realization that he had done contrary to Ileeta's express request of him, that he had dishonored her dying wish, that he had offended Ileeta's Jesus, who commanded a thing called forgiveness.

One day he left his lodge with a sack of pemmican and other provisions and rode down toward the Wichitas until he found the cairn under which he had laid Ileeta. He made camp nearby, then sat a long time in meditation, pondering the mystery. He spent the following day, and the day after, sitting, forcing his confused and inexperienced mind to dwell on Ileeta's god, and this god's demands upon those who revered him.

In Ileeta, Sanjak recognized, were qualities the names of which were not among the words he knew or used. Neither did he know their dimensions, but he recognized them to some degree in Brown Berry and Bird-that-Sings. There was loyalty and devotion, and contentment, an evenness of disposition and indifference to offense, a passive gratitude. All these the squaws had; but in Ileeta somehow they acquired a substance, a firmness, a strength that gave them an independent existence, demanding reverence of themselves—as a granite outcrop on the plain, like the Wichitas, was part of the earth, yet different from and apart from the common soil. About Ileeta Sanjak perceived dimly another presence, an overshadowing presence, like that of the Wichita heights seen through a mist, indistinct but substantial, one with the eye and gesture of authority, demanding obedience—and discipline, more exacting than that required to surmount the summit—a presence that he must propitiate if he would hold to the other. . . .

He was unable to dissolve the mist, to grasp the substance, the reality. Yet there was something he had learned, a path of action he knew he must follow. At the end of three days he broke camp and set out for his lodge.

Brown Berry and Bird-that-Sings recognized the change. His mood was cheerful, his insouciant humor had returned as had his playful affection toward the women. He resumed the hunt with renewed energy and saw to it that the lines were doubly filled with jerked meat, and while the squaws filled the pemmican bags, he strengthened the lodge poles and added new buffalo hides to the coverings. He also sold a string of his best ponies for silver and with it filled the pot from which they paid for meal and trinkets from the trader.

Then one day the squaws saw him carefully select a bow and a quiver of arrows and store them in a case of dressed antelope skin.

"You are going away?" asked Bird-that-Sings.

"Yes."

"Where do you go?"

"I go to seek the white men."

"Will you slay some of them?"

"No, I go only to see what the white man looks like, what he does, and why, and how."

"Will you take Spotted Horse Peter with you?"

"He is too young. You will guard him and feed him well until I return."

"Will you be gone long?"

"Do I know?"

"They say," continued Bird-that-Sings, "that the white man builds houses like those of the Pueblo Indians of the mesa country—but made not of earth. Will you see those?"

"Perhaps."

"And Yellow Flowers, she of Happy Owl's tepee, who is old and has seen much and hears more, says that the white man is now at peace with his brothers and is again building his iron trail into our hunting grounds. Is it so?"

"Yes, I have heard."

"The traders there, they say, have many things for the lodge, good knives, and copper pots, and beads and—"

But Brown Berry had begun to weep softly, leaning against Sanjak's knee and caressing it.

"You must not carry on," said Sanjak brusquely, at the same time putting his hand gently on her shoulder. "I will return."

Brown Berry was momentarily comforted.

"Will you bring back another white woman to the lodge?"

Sanjak laughed shortly, nervously. "Are not two enough? The tepee is small."

"Ileeta made you happy. She was good to have in this tepee. We could make room."

"No," said Sanjak shortly. "There will be only you and Bird-that-Sings."

It was an overcast day of early winter when Sanjak rode out of the camp, mounted on his piebald, a buffalo robe about his shoulders, a feather in his headband, his hair in two long braids tossing in the wind. Most of the camp was indoors; few saw him depart save Brown Berry and Bird-that-Sings, who stood at the lodge entrance and followed him with their eyes until he became a small figure in the sea of sere grass and finally disappeared over a rise.

"Will he come back?" asked Brown Berry, the tenderhearted one, and her eyes grew moist and a tear coursed down her brown cheeks.

"He will come back," assured Bird-that-Sings. "He is a Kiowa."

TWO

Sanjak did return. It was an afternoon of the second spring following his departure when some of the near-grown boys, not yet old enough for braves, playing handball in the field, saw a strange figure approaching across the prairie. He was riding a horse that, even at this distance, they recognized not to be an Indian pony, and he was not in Indian garb. In their eagerness to play the man they raced for their ponies and rode out to intercept him, keeping out of sight in the timber of the creek. Among them was the callow youth, Howling Dog, a nephew of Running Wolf and Running Wolf's only male relative.

It was Sanjak, mounted on a tall bay such as the white men bred, and crooked in his arm was one of the white men's rifles. On his head, instead of the feathered headband he wore a high, broad-brimmed felt hat, in the band of which, however, a feather had been thrust. His beaded doeskin shirt had given place to one of red flannel, and instead of breechclout and leggings, he wore corduroy pants.

It was a thinner Sanjak, too. There were lines in his face and his hands were calloused; his mood was sober. He was glad to be returning to his people, but the mystery he had sought to resolve still eluded him. The white men, he had found, were a strange mixture—with far wider differences among them in attitude, belief, and mood than among his own people. His people, and all their ways, he understood. The tepees in the distance, with the smoke curling from the lodge poles, had meaning, as did the herd of ponies grazing on the new spring grass: they spoke of movement and freedom, a freedom untrammeled by any restraint except one's mood.

Sanjak circled down by the woods that fringed the creek, through a field of wildflowers and past a clump of cottonwood, their downlike blossoms floating around him like a light snow. The Kiowas had a good land, he thought. If left alone by the white men, they should reach a peace with their unfriendly neighbors the Utes.

At that moment Sanjak felt a sudden tearing of his shirt and saw an arrow lodged in the cloth, missing his body by a finger breadth. At the same instant a shout arose from the creek bank, and a troop of half-grown boys appeared from the underbrush to rush out and surround him.

"Sanjak," they cried in welcome as they recognized him.

Sanjak drew out the arrow, examined it, and recognized the markings of Running Wolf. Running Wolf had not been a good craftsman; perhaps that was why the arrow had missed its mark.

"Whose among you is this?" he asked, and Howling Dog came forward.

"It was I," he said defiantly. "I knew you, for all your white man's furbishing. And I know about your wolf."

"You have a keen eye," responded Sanjak, and added grimly, "but I must teach you how to make arrows that fly

straight, and how to bend and draw the bow. You will come to
me and learn, but before you have learned and become a
brave, you will not again draw upon me. You have heard?"

The boy stood for a moment, uncertain, while the others
waited. Finally,

"I hear."

Turning to the others, Sanjak spoke.

"You have heard Howling Dog's words."

There was a responding assent.

"Then let us go on."

For some days Sanjak rested in his tepee. He was glad to be
alone in the company of his squaws, to savor again the jerked
beef, the marrow cakes, and the Indian stews they prepared,
to feel under him the soft wool of the buffalo robe, to watch his
son at play, toddling about on thick brown legs while Bird-
that-Sings prattled as the two women went about their work.
Their joy at having him again in the lodge was overfull, and
they showed him how abundantly they had cared for his son,
how neatly plaited and oiled was his hair, and how, well in
advance of his age, they had provided him with clothing to
wear—blue dyed breechclouts of doeskin, and doeskin leggings likewise of blue that fitted to his hips and were deco-
rated with beads and shells.

"Big boy. He has grown," Sanjak had commended the
squaws. "You have been good to the boy. Fed him well. You
had plenty to eat? No sickness?"

"No sickness. In two years he grows fast. We have missed
you. Spotted Horse Peter has missed you. You will stay home
now?"

Bird-that-Sings had wanted all the news, and for days Sanjak was required to give again and again an account of his
adventures.

"You have kept well?" Brown Berry asked, snuggling to
him after they had supped and Spotted Horse Peter was
asleep. "Nobody brought us word. We were very lonely."

"I kept well. I was busy. The white people work hard—very hard. I learned to work."

"What are the white men like?" asked Bird-that-Sings.

Sanjak laughed and pinched her.

"You are curious. Like Indians: some good, some bad. Like Indians, some think. Like Sanjak, some like to joke."

He chuckled.

"Trader Peacock played a big joke. I asked him for a paper to say to the white people that Sanjak is a good Indian. Instead, he writes that Sanjak is a bad Indian, to be beaten and driven away. And so I was beaten."

He went on to add,

"But the preacher who baptized Spotted Horse Peter came by just then, and gave me a job on railroad. Later I worked as smithy and learned to shoe horses, to mend wagons, to fashion knives and other things."

"Did you learn about Christians—which you went to learn?"

"Some things. Some things are still dark."

Presently,

"Are you becoming Christian?" asked Brown Berry.

Sanjak did not reply.

Brown Berry nestled closer.

"Did you find a Christian woman to bring to the lodge?" she asked.

"No one like Ileeta."

"How then shall we teach Spottled Horse Peter to be a Christian?"

Sanjak stirred uneasily.

"Christians have only one squaw. How can I bring a Christian woman to the lodge?"

Sanjak rose and went out, but presently returned. Seeing his unrest, Brown Berry said, "You still think of Ileeta." It was half statement, half question.

"Should I not?" demanded Sanjak brusquely. "She is the mother of our son."

"Would you not find another to bear you sons?"

"I am content," said Sanjak.

At this Bird-that-Sings spoke up.

"A certain brave of the Kiamish Kiowas has looked upon us with favor," she announced with a trace of assurance. "He has a hundred ponies. If you would have papooses, there would be room in the tepee if we left."

"Be quiet," growled Sanjak. "Said I not that he was our son? One bears, another feeds, and still another cuts and adorns the antelope skin for his back. He is ours."

"That pleases me," responded Bird-that-Sings.

"I shall be a white man in this," said Sanjak decisively. "Whether you bear or not, this is your lodge, as it is mine—and there shall be none other, save Brown Berry. I did not seek Ileeta. She was sent to me, even as you were sent to me."

"And by whom—and why?"

The question was innocent, perhaps casual, but it caused Sanjak to frown. He rose and went out. Dusk had fallen, and the west was a roseate flame that cast a glow on the lodges and the children playing in the dust. He walked toward the flame, as though to enter it, but the flame fled, as though to escape him, and he was in the open prairie, with the stars beginning to wink in the purple night. The breeze brought him the acrid odor of evening fires and the faint cries of the boys as they returned one by one to their tepees, and he was alone with his question: what was the meaning of her coming—and her swift going? For her, it had never been a question. Bird-that-Sings and Brown Berry had been sent to him by tribal custom. But for Ileeta, it was not custom but her god who had directed him to her, and she was obedient to her god's will, as she became obedient to Sanjak's will. What was this god, and what did he want of Sanjak?

It was a question still unresolved, which had risen again and again during his sojourn in the settlements, but which had found no definitive answer.

A memory deep within him struggled to surface—a memory as old as the first man, of having once met that god face-to-face and having held converse with him. Could he but disengage it, lift it from the murk within, and bring it to the light of day, he was sure he would know the secret of the mystery.

He did not know; at this moment he only knew that Spotted Horse Peter had been left him as a gage and token of the god's presence.

A star loosed itself and was hurled in a flaming streak across the sky. Sanjak saw its flight, saw it suddenly extinguished. He turned toward the tepee.

"It is for my son to know," he said to himself. "I must send him to Ileeta's god. And then, perhaps, he can tell me."

THREE

There were memories of his sojourn in the settlements that Sanjak did not relish, of which he was unwilling to talk, and which he tried to dismiss. But the talkative Bird-that-Sings, her curiosity piqued, continued to prod and eventually obtained the story.

"You have brought home a white man's rifle," she noted. "How did you get it?"

He was silent, but later Bird-that-Sings returned to the subject indirectly.

"You brought us no trinkets, as when you visit the trader." It was not a reproach, rather an avenue of curiosity, but it prompted Sanjak to reply.

"I left quickly. I had no time."

"Were they not good to you?"

"Yes—but I did not understand the white man's ways in council."

"You were in council?"

"It was as when one is brought before the elders for an offense against the tribe."

"Did you offend the white man?"

Again, Sanjak was silent, but then burst out,

"I killed a man."

"Did you count coup? Did you take his scalp?"

"It was not like that."

Reluctantly, Sanjak told them the story. While he was working as a smithy, the settlement bank was robbed. This, he explained, was where the white men kept their gold and silver. A war party was formed to pursue the robbers, and Sanjak was summoned to assist, with his greater Indian skill, in following the robbers' trail. They had fled into broken, hilly country, but the trail was easy for Sanjak, as one of the robbers had earlier brought his mount to have a cast shoe replaced. Sanjak had shod the horse, and he recognized his shoe marks in the turf.

"What is a horseshoe?" Brown Berry now asked, for the Kiowas wrapped their ponies' feet in leather.

Sanjak explained how the white men fastened iron to the feet with nails driven through the hoof, at which Brown Berry, the tenderhearted, shuddered.

Sanjak went on to tell how the posse, with Sanjak's aid, traced the robbers to a hideout—a cabin in a clearing—with scrub oak forest all around. The robbers, however, fired at anyone who showed himself in the clearing.

"These white men were not warriors. They did not understand battle," said Sanjak, "and they were afraid to take risks." He offered to creep around to the corral opposite, and while the posse made a diversion by firing and shouting he would dash in and open the corral gates and loose the horses. The robbers, then without means of flight, would surrender or be starved to submission.

Sanjak recalled suddenly that this was the way of the attack upon Santa Rosa that had brought him Ileeta, and for a moment he was lost in other memories, until Bird-that-Sings nudged him to continue.

"The robbers lodged here," explained Sanjak, making a mark on the earthen floor of the lodge, "and the horses are here in a corral. I crawl forward and wait for the posse to start firing, but one of the robbers comes out and walks toward the corral with a bucket of grain to feed the horses. He sees me, draws his gun, and fires. I fall down in the grass. The noise of his gun starts the posse firing, and the robber looks around. I rise and run to the corral, but the robber turns and fires again. By now I am at the edge of the corral and hide behind a post. I have my bow, and I fit an arrow and draw. The arrow goes straight, and the man falls. I now open the gate, and the horses run out into the woods. There is some more firing by the posse and by the robbers, and then they come out waving a white cloth and surrender.

"Afterward there is what is called a trial. A man sits on a high bench and listens. I am asked questions. But first they say I must be sworn."

" 'What does that mean?' I ask. They explain. I must first put my hand on the book and say I will tell the truth.

"I ask, 'What do you mean, tell the truth?' I am making a joke.

" 'Don't you know what truth is?' asks the man on the high bench.

" 'Sanjak always tells the truth,' I say. 'Why put my hand on the book? Is that medicine to make me tell the truth?'

" 'You just tell what you saw,' says the man on the high bench, 'and that will satisfy the court.'

"Then another man stands up and speaks to the man on the high bench. 'Your honor,' he says, and bows low, 'I object to this Indian telling what he saw. He's not capable of giving testimony in this case.'

" 'Why not?' asks the man on the high bench.

" 'First, he asks what is the truth, which shows he does not

113

know what truth is. Second, all Indians are liars and can't be trusted, even if he swears on the book. Besides, he can't swear on the book, for he's not a Christian.'

"Then there was much talk this side and that side, until the man on the bench finally says I can tell what I saw.

"Others also talk, and at the end the man on the bench says the robbers must hang. Many people come to see the hanging.

"But I go back to work in smithy and stay away."

Sanjak paused ruminatively.

"White men are peculiar," he commented. "Hard to understand."

He paused again while he recalled his bewilderment, and his eyes puckered.

"After a few days," he resumed, "the sheriff came to the smithy and arrested me. 'What for?' I ask.

" 'For killing a man,' the sheriff says.

"I say, 'You kill all the others with a rope. What's the difference in using an arrow?'

"The sheriff is very gentle. 'You don't understand, Sanjak,' he says. 'They were killed by law. You killed in self-defense. That is good excuse in law. But it is necessary for you to go before the judge—the man on the high bench—and explain. Then he will say you are innocent—that you did not kill the man—and then you go free. But just now I have to take you to jail until the judge comes and we have a trial. But don't worry, I will see you well fed.' "

Sanjak paused, and as he recalled the events he gave a chuckle.

"I don't like to stay in jail; I was in stockade once before. I tell the sheriff I cannot stay in jail. He says to me, 'Sanjak, you are a good Indian. You help catch the outlaws. Soon you will be free. Now you just walk in the yard, and only at night will I put you in cell.' But the yard is too small—not like the Indian hunting country."

"The cell is not locked," Sanjak concluded, "so one night I walk out, take the rifle on the wall, the horse in the stall, and ride back to the tribe."

The story pleased the squaws, and they said, "*Ai, ai,*" when Sanjak told how he left the settlements. It was a natural thing to do, as natural as for a deer to scamper off across the prairie once its tether had been removed.

FOUR

Sanjak had resumed his tribal dress, but his return in the garb of the white men and his absence among them had not been well received by the elders, whose attitude was a mixture of displeasure at Sanjak's abandonment of tribal tradition and a secret envy at his accomplishments—his new mastery of English, his acquaintance with the white man's customs and habits, and especially his acquisition of some of the white man's skills. Despite this ambivalence, however, he was welcomed in council, and at the moment there were grave matters to discuss.

Events had not gone well with the tribes during his absence. The white man's plow was steadily gnawing into traditional Indian lands; worse, the great herds of buffalo that were the meat and livelihood of the Indians were being slaughtered in great numbers by white hunters—by organized bands killing for the army, for the skins, or merely for sport. White men traveled the plains with tents and servants, shooting in rivalry as to who could bring down the greatest number in a day, until vast herds had disappeared and the plains were strewn with the bleached bones of their carcasses. To add to the unrest among the tribes were the armed forces that were patroling much of the plains where the Indians roamed, and there had been battles between bands of Indians and these roving patrols. There had also been unprovoked attacks upon Indian camps such as the one at Sand Creek, near the Great Mountains, when a large party of white men led by a certain Chivington fell upon the Cheyenne band of Chief Black Kettle, who had encamped his people near the fort under a guarantee of protection. Over two hundred old men, women, and children had been slaughtered and their scalps paraded in the streets of Denver mining town.

Recently there had appeared white emissaries in the camps—military chiefs in uniform, accompanied by horse soldiers, one bearing a white pennon in sign of amity; sometimes with them a man in a black coat that came to the knees and broad-brimmed black hat who was, he said, from the Society of Friends. They had brought presents, and they had asked about the condition of the tribes, the plentitude of game, whether any were sick or needed a doctor. They talked of a better relationship with what they called their "Indian brothers" and asked if the tribes would like a regular supply of sugar and beef, and would they for a price agree to keep their young men below the Arkansas and allow the white men to drive their cattle from Texas across their lands?

Finally they had announced that the Great White Father desired all the tribes to meet with his war chiefs at Medicine Lodge, at which the war chief of the white men would propose a settlement of all their differences and make a solemn treaty dividing the vast plains between them.

A solemn convocation of the chiefs of the Comanche and

117

THE KIOWA

Kiowa peoples was held, in which there was great debate whether to meet with the white men or no. The chiefs assembled in a big lodge especially made for the purpose, large enough to hold the two score chiefs and elders who attended. After greetings and small talk, and after the pipe had been smoked around the circle, old Cow-with-a-Hump, the eldest and most highly respected, though chief of the lesser Kiowas, began the discussion by stating the issue. Several raised questions about this or that. Did anyone know the white man's mind? How should the land be divided? What would be the boundaries? Indecision prevailed until Buzzard Quill, the noted warrior and principal chief of the Kwahadi Comanches, stood up and, advancing to the fire in the center of the lodge, waited for silence. He had come in his war regalia and amulets, and now, laying aside his feathered headdress, began to speak.

"What do the white men want?" he asked. "They wish to put us in a corral as they put their horses, where they can throw their lasso around each one in turn and lead it forth until all are gone—then they will burn down the corral. I have spoken to the white men. What do they seek? I will tell you. They ask that we allow the iron road to pass through our lands. If you have seen their machines of the trail, breathing fire and belching smoke so that the sky is clouded and we choke on the dust, and roaring like a spring storm that breaks down the forest and overturns our tepees—if you have seen and heard these monsters, your answer will be no.

"What else do they want? They ask that we do not hunt north of the Cimarron and do not cross the Red River into Texas, that we do not trouble the Texans when they drive their cattle north through our lands, eating our grass as they travel."

He paused, and one of the chiefs spoke up, inquiring respectfully.

"And what do the white men give in exchange?"

Buzzard Quill made a gesture of contempt.

"They offer to give us houses made of wood, which can not

be moved like a tepee, as when we follow the buffalo. What would befall? Our camps would become a field of offal and debris. We could no longer move from our droppings, as do the buffalo, and let the sun and the wind and the rain purify the earth. In this the white men are very strange."

He gave a grimace.

"Besides this, they will give us pieces of iron by which we should tear up the earth on which the Great Spirit has planted grass and instead sow some seeds of the white man's giving, while the upturned earth lies like a naked squaw, to be raped and carried away by every wind that blows, by every falling rain.

"This land is ours. In the days of the forefathers we traveled from the Arkansas to the great river beyond which lies the land of the Mexicans. We were called the Lords of the Plains. No tribe challenged us, no tribe trespassed but at its peril. Save only the Cheyennes, no people sent greater warriors into battle."

He paused and concluded,

"For me and my people, we will not meet the white man."

The Kwahadi Comanches ranged the high plains toward the Great Mountains and so far had not been troubled by trespass as had the other bands whose hunting grounds were closer to the intruding settlements.

"Buzzard Quill's words are like milk to a hungry papoose," commented Cow-with-a-Hump. He was ancient and cautious. "But can they grow warriors in sufficient number to make war?"

"Let them make war!" cried Buzzard Quill defiantly. "Better to die in battle than by digging the earth like the Cherokees."

There were further speeches, some one way, some another, until Cow-with-a-Hump, in some weariness, spoke again.

"We have not heard the words of Sanjak, who has been among the white men and has learned much. What is your counsel?"

Sanjak, now bidden to speak, removed his headdress and

took his place by the fire. Before speaking, he stooped down and gathered a handful of twigs, which he broke one by one and cast on the coals. He now gathered another handful, which he bound together with a thong drawn from his antelope shirt. He handed the bundle to one of the younger men near the fire. "Break," he commanded, as one after another tried but failed against the flexible twigs.

He now addressed the company.

"Our people are as these twigs," he began. "We are puny before the white man because we are divided. The Pawnees fight the Cheyennes and the Osage the Apaches. Few are the brotherhoods among us—such as the Kiowa and the Comanche, or the Cheyenne and the Arapahoe. The white men are again as one people. It is useless to treat with the white men unless we are agreed to a common end. Buzzard Quill speaks for the Kwahadis. But what of the Kotsoteka or the Nokini? Are our brothers the Comanches of one mind among themselves? Is our brother and elder Buzzard Quill such a voice as to call all the bands of the Comanches to council?"

Without waiting for answer Sanjak continued.

"While I have lived among the white men, I am a Kiowa. The white men are strange. I do not understand them. But I have given much thought to the matter. Among them are men who wish peace with the Indians, who do not agree to the war path. They call themselves Christians, and while I do not understand their worship, I found much good will among them."

Suddenly, in the midst of his address, as he spoke of the Christians, a great cloud of memory enclosed him so that he no longer saw the walls of the lodge, the fire burning in the center, the circle of oiled and copper-colored faces gleaming in the firelight. For a moment he seemed to the elders to be lost in an abstraction, in an attitude of listening, as though hearing some message given him by a spirit speaking through the walls of the lodge, heard by him alone.

Sanjak recovered himself, and then in a gesture familiar only to the Plains Indians, and then only when they stood in

council on weighty matters, and asserted what they solemnly
held in conviction—Sanjak dropped his apron and stood
before the elders in his naked and unadorned majesty of
manhood—the highest gage he could offer for the redemption
of his words.

"I have known these Christians," he said solemnly. "One of
them dwelt in my lodge, and is the mother of my only son—
Ileeta, whom you remember. She was a woman of peace, and
for her sake I went among the white men to learn the way of
peace. And among them I met many who wish to live in peace
with us, whom they call 'our Indian brothers.'

"If we are wise, O elders, we will counsel our people to
accept the white man's offer and to attend his council."

Sanjak's counsel was seconded by Kicking Bird, chief of
one of the smaller bands of the Kiowas, and when it was
learned that Black Kettle of the Cheyennes, whose band had
been slaughtered at Sand Creek, was despite this treachery
also of the peace party, the council concluded that the Comanches and Kiowas should go to Medicine Lodge.

FIVE

In accordance with the treaty with the white men, the Comanches and Kiowas were restricted to the territory south of the Washita River and north of the Red. Sanjak's band of Kiowas now set up their lodges on Rainy Mountain Creek, which flowed out of the granite uplift of the Wichitas. Despite the fact that the land was good, the grass plentiful, and the water abundant, the people were unhappy, remembering the days of freedom when they hunted the buffalo from the Great River to the Great Mountains and made war in the springtime and raids on the settlements. They complained now about the beef carcasses the government commissary distributed among them at periodic intervals; and the younger braves, seeking to get a name for themselves like their elders, dared from time to time the prohibitions of the white men and went across the Red River to gain horses and scalps.

Sanjak had accepted the restrictions on movement with the assent of one who retreats into an inner world of memory of former days. At the same time, he sank back more and more into the tribal ways and tribal habits of thought. He was content to spend his days before his lodge in meditation, in memories—recalling Ileeta, and her quiet way, her tenderness, her solicitude—qualities that were new to him in those days, but qualities he had met with also in varying degree in the settlements, the Svensons in particular, but others also. He found much happiness also in watching his son grow up, and in him he could see again the boy's mother, and he loved the lad with a love that also was new and strange to him.

Once he climbed among the rocks to find the place where Ileeta lay, and he sat beside the cairn of stones for a day; but he did not return again. Ileeta was not there; she was somewhere else; earth itself could not hold her.

Just now Sanjak was in the pasture where some of his herd of ponies grazed, and he was teaching Spotted Horse Peter the mastery of horses. With them was young Howling Dog, to whom Sanjak, as he had promised, was teaching the arts of war and hunt, and who had come to accept Sanjak as his patron. It was late in the afternoon, and as they left off to return to the lodge, they saw a vehicle on the distant horizon. It was a buggy drawn by a pair of mules. The top was down, and as it drew near, Sanjak saw in it a white man holding the reins and an Indian sitting beside him. Sanjak rode out to greet the visitor. The Indian, Sanjak noted, was a Caddo.

"Tell this chief—for such I take him to be," began the man speaking to the Caddo, "—that I am Joseph Makin, the agent sent out by the Great White Father to be a protector and guide to our Indian brothers."

As he spoke, he wrapped the reins around the whipstock and climbed down and extended his hand, at the same time removing his broad-brimmed flat hat. Sanjak got down from his pony. The agent, he noted, was of stocky build and somewhat shorter than himself, with a rotund face, clear blue eyes, and a bald head. His expression was pleasant, and he smiled as he spoke.

"I can speak English—some," said Sanjak. "You are welcome. I am Sanjak, hunting chief of the Nut Eaters."

"I have heard of you—as one who knows the white man and would walk the white man's road."

"The sun will soon go away," said Sanjak. "Your mules are tired. You will lodge with Kiowas."

"You are gracious," said the agent.

Sanjak was acquainted with the word *gracious* but not precisely with what it meant.

"Not gracious, just Kiowa," he responded.

The agent smiled.

"Good Kiowa," he exclaimed, and Sanjak knew he would like him.

Sanjak took Makin to his own lodge, which the squaws had vacated after serving the supper.

"I give you Kiowa food," said Sanjak. "Maybe you like it, maybe not."

"I shall like it," responded Makin.

"This is what the white men call 'jerky,' " explained Sanjak. "Buffalo meat dried in sun, then soaked in water to soften it and afterward put on coals of fire."

Accompanying it was a cake the agent tasted and then looked inquiringly. Sanjak explained that it was made of marrow cooked with crushed sweet mesquite beans. There were sweet cakes made, Sanjak also explained, of persimmon paste and pulped hackberries, mixed with fat and ground nuts and roasted on the end of a stick. Finally there was coffee obtained from the government store.

Before eating, Sanjak, following his tribal custom, took a piece of meat and buried it in a small hole in the earth, which he made with the point of his knife. He observed that the agent bowed his head for a moment, and suddenly the memory of the Svensons returned to him.

"You are a Christian?" asked Sanjak.

"Yes. Quaker."

"You say prayer for lodge," said Sanjak.

The agent again bowed his head and gave a short thanksgiving.

"Good. Now we eat."

The agent, Sanjak noted, partook with goodwill, if not with relish, and betrayed his unfamiliarity with Indian diet only by brushing off the cinders and ash from the meat before eating. Sanjak thought the ash good for the stomach.

Afterward, Sanjak, Makin, and the Caddo sat about the fire—it was early spring and the nights were cool—and Sanjak passed around his pipe. Makin accepted and only coughed a little as he drew in the acrid smoke. Spotted Horse Peter was also in the lodge, sitting solemnly silent on the buffalo robe behind Sanjak.

Makin liked to talk, and he had a great curiosity.

"I am a farmer," he explained. "I know little about your way of life. But I must learn. You must tell me about how you live, what you do."

"What we do?" asked Sanjak, laughing. "Indian do what he likes. If he like sun, he go sit in sun. If he like shade, he sit in shade. When hungry, he go hunting. When cold, he put on buffalo robe. Good life. You like to ride? We have many ponies. Good to ride. Makes man feel good."

It was now Makin's turn to laugh.

"Do you know what farming is?"

"I have seen."

Memories of his experience in the settlements when he was set to digging postholes returned to Sanjak, and he grimaced.

"It also is a good life, when you get used to it," commented Makin, noting the grimace, and let it go at that.

"You placed a portion of your meat in the earth. May I ask why?"

"Our medicine men say this is a gift to Earth Spirit. Earth our mother, they say. We take food from the earth as papoose takes milk from mother's breast. Sky our father, who sends us sun to warm us, rain to cool us—sometime storm in anger, like chief whose son does not go on the right path."

"It is good to give thanks," asserted Makin. "Do you talk with Mother Earth and Father Sky?"

Sanjak laughed uneasily.

"Much talk, not much answer. Earth too busy, I think."

"Do you have questions to ask—or things to ask for?"

Sanjak drew up proudly. "What do I need to ask for? Plenty meat, plenty fire, squaws—son." He hesitated, his broad bronze face drawn at the corners. "But questions—many," he added.

"What sort?" prodded the agent.

Sanjak found difficulty in replying. He himself did not know what his questions were. He only knew he was continually aware of distant memories so elusive as never to be captured but persistently drawing him on toward inchoate longings that took various shapes and directions and continually evaded capture in words or meanings.

"We ask our medicine," he said, avoiding the question. "Medicine tell when time is good for hunting, when time is good for moving camp, when time is good for smoking pipe in council."

"Tell me about your medicine," asked Makin.

"We have big medicine for tribe. Medicine man carry it. Keep it in leather sack. Other medicine belong to brave, sometime, if he lucky. I have good Medicine."

For a moment, finding the agent a man with whom he could talk and whom he could trust, Sanjak was about to draw out, from where it hung by a thong about his neck, sewed up in leathern sack, the crucifix that had been Ileeta's. But he had shown no man his Medicine, and a grave hesitancy held him now. The Medicine had been good to him—he had suffered no ailment in his years, no arrow or bullet had struck him, his pony had never stumbled in a prairie dog hole, his teeth were yet sound, his eyesight keen, his hearing unimpaired. All this, without doubt, he owed to the protection of his Medicine.

But there was the mystery beyond his comprehension—

how a man dead with hands and feet and belly pierced, and hung on a cross, could live again; how further, as Ileeta had assured him, this man not only lived but would, by her faith, bring her to life again. And others having faith—Sanjak included—he would raise from death. It was too much, too mysterious, too wonderful for belief. He had hoped it might be true, for the memory and vision of Ileeta was forever before his eyes, yet it was beyond his simple experience, too much to believe. Had it been a spirit descending in a clap of thunder, that was one thing, but a mere man, and the man dead—that was another.

It was, he vaguely sensed, like that living world to be found beneath the waters of a stream that cannot be seen for the rippling of the surface, yet is visible when the surface becomes calm. Perhaps if he could but quiet the motions of his spirit until he could become utterly still, he could then see past the surface of being into the mysteries of eternal being. . . .

But that was too much for his simple nature. He kept silence on the subject of his Medicine. Makin, sensing the depth of his reticence, turned to another subject of his curiosity.

"Your son?" nodding to Spotted Horse Peter.

"My son," said Sanjak proudly.

"How old?"

"Nine summers."

Makin regarded the lad more closely and noted the round eyes so different from the angular slits of the father's, the complexion dark rather than ruddy, and the abundance of black hair.

"Mother Kiowa?" he asked, puzzled, half-probing.

"Mother Mexican woman."

The agent had seen Bird-that-Sings and Brown Berry in the lodge, and it was obvious that they were not Mexican. His brow gathered in perplexity, but he hesitated to explore the mystery. Yet with innocent curiosity he persisted.

"Mother—here?" he asked.

"Mother dead," said Sanjak.

"I'm sorry," said Makin.

"You read?" asked Sanjak to ease his guest.

"Yes, I read."

"That's good."

"In fact, I plan to start a school."

"That's better. I send Spotted Horse Peter."

Makin brightened.

"That's the best news yet. Spotted Horse Peter? What an interesting name. How was he named Peter?"

"Mother name him. Mother Christian. Grow up Christian. Good Christian. She want Spotted Horse Peter to be Christian. You make him?"

"That," said the agent softly, "is why I came to this land. But we do not make Christians. Only the Great Spirit makes Christians. We pray that many be led to desire the gift."

He turned to Spotted Horse Peter.

"May I speak to the lad?"

Sanjak called the boy.

"Do you know what it is to go to school?"

Sanjak translated. The boy nodded. Sanjak had often spoken to him of the white man's school.

"Would you like to come to my school?" asked the agent.

The boy gave his answer, and Sanjak burst into laughter.

"He says, 'Sometime. Not all time. Go hunting sometime.' "

The agent now chuckled.

"Good. I wouldn't want that myself. 'All work and no play,' they say, 'makes Jack a dull boy.' We will start school in a fortnight at the Indian Agency. I have a good man coming then. Bring the boy. We will have books, slate, crayons."

SIX

At Agent Makin's urging, the Nut Eaters had moved camp to Medicine Creek, not far from the agency, and the agency brought carpenters who erected a number of frame houses for their occupancy. Sanjak accepted one of them, but his example was followed by only one or two of the elders. The remainder kept to their tepees. The house had two rooms, an iron stove, two glass windows, and a pine floor. It was surrounded by several acres of land, which were supposed to be cultivated, but which Sanjak used to graze his ponies. The house was comfortable in winter, but when spring came, Sanjak, for all his previous experience in the settlements, suffocated, and the squaws grumbled about the heat, and he moved to a tepee. The agent was disappointed, for he had

hoped that many of the Indians would follow Sanjak's example and take to settled living, but the few who had done so
now followed Sanjak to the open fields. Sanjak explained to
the agent that he needed more ground to graze his ponies.

Hunting was getting steadily harder. There were few buffalo, and other game was scarce, but some venison was avail-
able in the hills, and the fishing was rewarding. Kiowas never
fished, but Sanjak was willing to learn and now often went
fishing with Spotted Horse Peter, and as the boy was growing
up they talked more freely together. Spotted Horse Peter,
along with several other Kiowa boys, had been attending the
school Makin had started. Father and son were speaking in
abbreviated English.

"How you like going to school?" Sanjak asked.

"Good. I like."

"What you learn at school?"

Spotted Horse Peter squinted, looked at the sky, and
thought.

"I learn writing."

"That's good. What do you write?"

Spotted Horse Peter thought, then brightened.

"I can read," he said, evading the question.

Sanjak slapped his thigh in satisfaction.

"Good. Very good. White man have many books, lots to
read. You learn much in books. What else you learn?"

Spotted Horse Peter explained in Kiowa as best he could
the mysteries of arithmetic and geography and government.
Geography Sanjak understood the value of: it was good to be
able to look at a piece of paper and know where one was, if one
did not know already, or how to get to a certain place where
one had not been before.

"What else?"

Spotted Horse Peter had about exhausted the curriculum.

"They teach you how to make tepee?" asked Sanjak. "No?
How to make fire in rain and wind? No? How to track deer and
small game? No? How to dry meat so that it does not spoil but
keep good all winter? No? How to flay deer and remove hair

and make skin soft like cotton? No?"

Sanjak straightened up, giving his attention to his fish line. They were on the edge of a limpid pool, filled from a spring farther up in the hills. A twig from an overbranching willow tree fell into the water and set ringlets expanding on the glassy surface. Sanjak considered this phenomenon without analyzing its why or wherefore, then turned to Spotted Horse Peter.

"What they tell you about being Christian?"

"They don't say. They say how a Christian behave."

"You already Christian. When baby, you were baptized. That make you Christian—I think. Like being initiated into Red Legs. But you can be a Red Leg and not be a Red Leg, especially if you don't go on raids. And be initiated Christian and not be Christian. How does Christian behave?"

"Agent Makin talk to us—many times. Over and over he say, 'Christians don't lie,' 'Christians don't steal,' 'Christians don't take other man's wife,' 'Christians not lazy, but work.' " Spotted Horse Peter suddenly arrested his catalog. "What is work?" he asked.

Sanjak grimaced, then laughed.

"Work is doing what you don't like to do because somebody say you must."

"If you like it, then it not work?"

"No, it is fun, then, or a game—like fishing. What else he say?"

Spotted Horse Peter thought.

"Good Christians don't drink white man's firewater. Why, if white men Christian, they make firewater?"

Sanjak regarded his son solemnly.

"Remember this—not all white men Christian, even though they say so. Wise Indian learn to know who is good Christian, who not."

There were other dilemmas about the Christian way of life, one of which arose later when they had returned to the lodge.

"Agent says Christians have only one wife," remarked Bird-that-Sings in the middle of her chatter about nothing.

THE KIOWA

Sanjak was sitting at the door of the lodge, enjoying the evening air and the rays of the afternoon sun, while he smoked a pipe filled with agency tobacco. He had been only half-listening, his thoughts on distant memories. He now turned sharply.

"When did the agent say that?"

But he knew. Agent Makin, in addition to starting a school for the children who would attend, was holding classes for such of the Indian women who wished to come, to learn some of the household arts of the white women, including sewing, mending, simple cookery. The lessons were given by the agent's wife, a plain woman with a placid disposition, along with a good humor and patience needed to bear up under the vagaries of the Indian temperament. At these sessions Agent Makin always took opportunity to hold a five- or ten-minute homily on his favorite theme, the duty of a Christian.

"You wish to send me away?" asked Bird-that-Sings, busying herself with her pots.

"You don't go away," said Sanjak shortly. "Never mind those Kiamish braves. Anyway, you're too old."

"Brown Berry maybe?"

"Nor Brown Berry. Both stay here."

Bird-that-Sings went on with her work, while she turned her tongue to other matters.

"Agent has taught a new song. Would you like to hear?"

Sanjak, half-listening, assented.

"It says,

> Jesus love me—
> This I know,
> For the Bible tells me so.

"You like it?"

Bird-that-Sings had a melodious voice, and if her pronunciation made it hard to understand the words, at least they were sung with spirit.

"I like."

Bird-that-Sings prattled on but presently returned to her concern.

"You don't wish to be a Christian?" she asked.

"Why do you ask?"

"You tell Spotted Horse Peter all the time, 'Must not steal,' 'Must not tell lie.' You don't tell lie. You don't steal—at least I think so. Why don't you want one squaw, like the white man?"

"Because I have two squaws," responded Sanjak testily. "How shall I send one away?"

"You want to see Ileeta again. How will you see her if you don't go to the Christian after-place?"

"You talk too much, woman," said Sanjak irritably, and rose and left the lodge. Again he walked upon the prairie, but he saw neither the hawk that circled in the sky nor the prairie dog sitting on the edge of his hole, munching on some roots of blue stem while warily watching the hawk. These questions were too much for Sanjak's limited experience in probing the mysteries of the metaphysical. He saw no solution to his dilemma.

Presently he returned to the lodge. Bird-that-Sings was still working at her bead embroidery, another butter-soft piece of deerskin for a jacket for Spotted Horse Peter.

"Don't speak again about being a Christian. I don't go where you don't go," said Sanjak gruffly.

Bird-that-Sings fell into contented silence, but Sanjak remained in uncomfortable dilemma. A short time thereafter he proposed to the Nut Eaters that camp be moved westward to Rainy Mountain Creek, where, he said, the buffalo were more abundant.

However, he consented to let Spotted Horse Peter remain at the agency and attend the agency school, residing in the dormitory that had been erected for the purpose.

SEVEN

Much as he was taken by the agent's teaching about Christianity, there were other things about the white man's road that increasingly troubled Sanjak—and not him alone but others among the tribe. They grew more and more reluctant to come to the agency for the rations distributed by the white men, until at last Agent Makin sent word that he would visit the tribe and hear their grievances. A council was arranged on Rainy Mountain Creek to which the elders of the principal bands of both Kiowas and Comanches were summoned. Among them were Yellow Horse, White Cloud, old Cow-with-a-Hump, and Sanjak of the Kiowas; and Buzzard Quill, Tall Man, and Limping Pony of the Comanches, together with lesser personages of the bands.

The agent came alone, accompanied only by his Caddo

interpreter, but this time in an army ambulance fitted with mattress for sleeping and a camp stove for cooking. Evidently he sensed that his welcome would be cold. And it was so, that even when they were some distance away, the dogs rushed out and set up a ferocious yelping about his mules' heels. They were driven away by boys dispatched by the chiefs who, when Makin drove up, were assembled before a larger lodge. They received the agent gravely and reservedly, and after offering him food invited him to speak.

"Brothers," he began, "for some time the Great Father in Washington—who himself in his day was a noted warrior, the greatest among his people—has been sad over the condition of his Red children. Two years ago he sent his chiefs to make a peace between his white children and his Red. To assure his Red children of his good intentions, he has appointed men of peace as his agents with the several tribes. We are Quakers, that is, of a Christian sect known as the Society of Friends. The first of us Quakers, a man named William Penn, came to the land of the Red men two hundred years ago. He made a treaty of peace with the Indians. That treaty has never been broken. We Quakers do not believe in war; we believe in peace. We hope that you will accept my assurance that I have come only to serve your welfare."

This speech was translated by the Caddo, who had a better knowledge of English than Sanjak, but less of the Comanche. The chiefs meditated upon what was said, and nodded in understanding, but maintained their reserve.

"If I am to serve you," continued Makin, "you must come to the agency, as I am only one man to go among so many. Beef and sugar and coffee and blankets, as agreed to by the treaty, await you there. Some of you have come from time to time, but many remain away. If any of you have complaints, I am here to listen and, within my power, to remove them."

When this was translated, Buzzard Quill, the firebrand and opponent to dealing with the white men, rose to speak on behalf of the Comanches. He began in a courteous and conciliatory vein.

"Our hearts were filled with joy when you came among us to show us the white man's road," he began, "even as the water courses are filled by the coming of the spring rains. We rejoiced as the cattle when the grass springs afresh from its winter sleep. We had heard of you as one who loved his brother man and especially his Indian brothers of the plains, and we were not disappointed. And now we look for blessing from our present meeting, and as we behold you, our faces light with joy.

"We have turned our ways, as you know, to follow the white man's road. But the way has been made hard, and we are glad that you have come that we may have a talk on these matters.

"From the Arkansas to the Red River extend the lands the Great White Father promised to the Indians as their home forever—for the Kiowas and Comanches the territory south of the Washita; that north of the Washita to the Cheyennes and Arapahoes; and the lands to the east to the Osages, the Wichitas, the Apaches, and the Caddoes. In these lands the Indians might dwell, untroubled by the white men, and the white men were forbidden to hunt the buffalo or to trespass.

"We now see the white men making lines, setting up stones, and driving stakes with marks on them. We do not know what it means, but our young men question and say, 'It is not good.'

"Why have the white men now made a fort with many soldiers near Medicine Creek that flows out of the Wichita Mountains near the agency to which you would have us come? It is for that that our people are afraid to come to the agency for the presents promised us.

"The white man's words were at first sweet as the mesquite bean, but now like green persimmons. As the Comanches take antelope by driving them into a circle of hunters, so the white men draw a line upon the earth and say to the Indian, 'Enter.' The White Father has said he would build us houses, but we do not want them. We were born under the sky, with the wind upon our faces and the sun upon our backs, and everywhere the air was clean. We want to die under the sky and not under the roof of a house or behind a wall. So why do you ask us to leave our happy waters, our free winds, and the warming sun? Speak no more of it."

It was a a long speech, and interrupted from time to time as the Caddo translated, and punctuated by grunts of approval by the other chiefs.

Makin listened to this address with respect and interest, and when Buzzard Quill finished, he closed and laid aside his notebook into which he had been entering notes. Rubbing his bald pate thoughtfully, he indicated that he would speak.

"I rejoice," he began, "that my good friend Buzzard Quill has on behalf of his Indian brothers spoken, for there is a road from heart to heart, and when men travel that road, they sleep in peace. Between my heart and that of Buzzard Quill the road is wide and well traveled. I hope it may be so with each of you.

"Let me first speak of the soldiers at Fort Sill. They are under my command, and I have forbidden them to harm or touch any of our Red brothers. There are, as you say, certain white men who trespass upon the land assigned to the tribes. In the markets of the East buffalo hides now fetch a good price, and many are tempted by the lure of gain to trespass upon the reservations. The soldiers are here to protect the Indians from such trespass. As for the men driving stakes, that is for one purpose or another, relating to the Indians' good. Some are for houses—for if the Kiowas and Comanches do not wish to live in houses, others of the tribes have found them comfortable—the Caddoes and the Wichitas, for instance. Some stakes are being driven to mark the way for the iron road, which will bring the abundance of treaty goods with swiftness rather than by the weary way of wagons.

"And now, let me speak of other matters. I repeat, the soldiers at Sill are under my command, and that command is to befriend and to protect, not to harass. But across the Red River in Texas are other soldiers not under my command, and they have orders that if any Indian bands make raids into Texas, they may pursue them so far as need be to punish them.

"I beg you, therefore, that you speak to your young men and forbid them to go raiding into Texas, or beyond into Mexico, as has been reported."

Makin now turned the talk to other matters. He spoke of the quantities of beef and coffee and sugar and blankets that were awaiting them at the agency, and prayed that the chiefs on reflection would have their people come in and receive them. He also spoke of houses that would be erected for those who wished them, and hoped that despite Buzzard Quill's defense of tepee life they would consent to dwell in them; he spoke also of seeds and plows for those who would return to the ancient habits and till the soil. And finally he spoke of the school he had opened and urged them to send their young boys and girls for instruction.

When all this had been translated, there was a consultation among the chiefs, and then Buzzard Quill replied.

"We have listened to your words. Your heart is good, and our hearts are warm toward you. You ask us to restrain our young men from crossing into Texas for cattle. That is good. But we are but chiefs, and young men listen to their chiefs no more than the young men of the white man listen to their elders. The agent, however, has at his command many soldiers, and no doubt when he has prevented the unruly young men of his people from trespassing on the reserved lands, we may be able to persuade our young men to leave off the war paint.

"Still," he concluded, "let us understand each other. We will travel the road between our hearts. Let us smoke. The agent will sleep with us tonight, and tomorrow he shall return in safety to the agency."

EIGHT

Sanjak had ridden into the agency to see how Spotted Horse Peter was doing in school and to bring him some furred shirts and other garments against the coming of winter. They had been made by Brown Berry, the quieter of the two squaws, who said little but whose nimble fingers, while Bird-that-Sings chattered, were the more assiduously employed in making this or that for Spotted Horse Peter. More than Bird-that-Sings, after Ileeta's death, she had in her silent and unnoticed way taken Ileeta's place as mother to the boy.

The school stood at a distance of a hundred yards or so from the main agency structure. Like the agency, it was a long, low building, half sod, half timber, half-set in the slope of the prairie, a semidugout, with a roof of grassy sod. One end was the schoolroom; the other served as sleeping quarters for the boys. There were as yet no girls in attendance.

Sanjak found his son playing with several others in the open yard. It was a game that resembled one played by the squaws and young girls: it was like kick-the-ball, which was done by hopping on one foot and with the other kicking a round leather ball stuffed with deer hair. There were differences in this new game, yet so few that one might say they were playing women's game. It was a good game; indeed, in the days of the fathers, it was still played by boys, but in more recent times it had been reserved for the squaws and young girls, and men who played it were called squaws. Sanjak thought that the schoolmaster must be very good that he could entice his pupils to such a game; he liked it that they were willing to challenge the tribal convention. At a break in the play he called his son to him.

"You like this game?"

"Yes, father."

Sanjak liked even better his son calling him father. Though he had always demanded and obtained the respect due a father, it was the custom that he be called by his proper name; there was something warming to be addressed as father.

"You still like school?"

He was speaking in English, to test his own and his son's proficiency in the language. The boy nodded.

"Good."

"But I would go on buffalo hunt."

"Buffalo hunt over. Soon snow, and we make camp warm for winter. It is warm in schoolhouse?"

"Too warm."

"You stay. Good for boy to learn."

"Some boys leave. They go by night. They go on warpath with braves. Do you go on warpath?"

"I walk the white man's road. But some foolish braves go. Not much buffalo. They take cattle from across river. Sometimes other things. Not good. You stay here. Good."

"I stay."

"Good."

Sanjak gave his son the shirts, leggings, and new moccasins made by the squaws, and then went on to the agency. Here he found the usual hangers-on—Caddoes, Wichitas, and others of the tribes that had for some years followed the white man's road and now dressed in pants, woolen shirts, and tall felt hats into the bands of which feathers were often thrust—nostalgic mementos of an abandoned past. There were few Kiowas or Comanches about the agency, Sanjak noted. They could be identified, if not by their stocky frames, their broad faces, and their lordly walk, by their retention of traditional dress. If some of them consented to abandon the apronlike breechclout in favor of the white man's garment, they would cut out the seat of the pants—it would be to waste the cloth, they explained, in riding to put it between a man's buttocks and his pony.

The agency was a long building, one end of which served as the agent's living quarters, the middle as his office, and the other end as the storeroom for the government treaty rations—when there were rations. The storeroom was generally empty, and when shipments did arrive, there were the eager Caddoes and Wichitas to take their allotments at once, leaving little for the wandering tribes. To their protests Agent Makin explained that it was the fault of the government contractors in not making regular deliveries, and he had protested often to Washington—but without success.

The agent saw Sanjak from his window and hurried to welcome him to his office.

"It is good to see my brother," he exclaimed. "I have much to say to you, and our hearts must speak to each other."

"Hard for hearts to speak when bellies empty. Much unhappiness among my people."

"It is of that of which I would speak. Tell your young men that as the elders have smoked the pipe of peace with the white men, they must learn patience. I have not been able to provide the rations with the changes of the moon, but as you see I have kept the soldiers to their quarters."

He pointed through the window toward Fort Sill. It lay a mile distant, a low collection of stone barracks, with frame houses for officers, and stone corrals, and stables. Apart from smoke curling from the barracks chimneys, there was little evidence of human activity.

"Their commander Colonel Grierson tells me that the Comanches continue to go into Texas and drive off cattle and ponies, and sometimes seize women and children, whom they ransom with the traders for whiskey, tobacco, or rifles. He says they must punish these bad men, but I have said, 'Let us be patient for a while. When the wagons bring the rations with the change of the moon, then will be time to send the soldiers after the young men.'"

"You have spoken from the heart, and you know the heart of the Indian," said Sanjak. "But tell the soldiers to drive away the white hunters of the buffalo, and there will be meat for the lodges, and no need to raid the ranches."

"We are brothers, Sanjak. Let us remain so. We cannot forbid the storm to come, but we can warn against the wrath. And now let me speak of the Cheyennes. You are a friend of Black Kettle, I understand."

"Yes, friend. Kiowas are not brothers to the Cheyennes— but friends, yes. Black Kettle I know. Black Kettle is a wise and good chief."

"Would he listen to you, you think?"

"I listen to Black Kettle," said Sanjak modestly.

"If it were something important?"

"Maybe."

"There is bad, bad blood between the Cheyennes and the army. Some Cheyennes have fought battles with hunters, and some white men were killed. The army says it must punish the Cheyennes. Agent Habercord, my colleague, is helpless. Regrettably, the army will not listen to him.

"You have heard of General Yellow Hair, who wears a white hat and rides a white stallion—the one who became famous for his raids during the war between the white men?"

Yes. Sanjak had heard of the cavalry officer who wore his

yellow hair to his shoulders, who was fond of flamboyant uniforms, and who was noted for the swiftness and savagery of his campaigns. He had become the principal antagonist of the northern tribes, the Sioux in particular.

"They have ordered Yellow Hair and his cavalry regiment here to control the Cheyennes, and if I have my guess, Yellow Hair will not be gentle, as is Colonel Grierson with the Kiowas and Comanches. If Black Kettle is your friend, then go and tell him and his people to be quiet and patient and not to give further occasion or excuse for the army to move."

Sanjak thought. It was true, as the agent had said, that conditions were different in the Cheyenne reservation. Despite Black Kettle's influence and his control over his own band of Amarillo Cheyennes, the tribe was restive; the Cheyennes had not forgotten their Colorado lands, which they had surrendered for this reservation on the Oklahoma prairie, and they preferred to hunt there, where the buffalo were still to be had. But it was also a land into which white settlers were pressing, both for tillage and mining, and where the white hunters were particularly active.

"Black Kettle is a man of peace, but other Cheyennes are very unhappy. I will talk to Black Kettle," said Sanjak.

NINE

The weather had turned cold; there was the smell of snow in the overcast sky, and a raw north wind whined in the dry grass and through the groves of blackjack along the creek. The Cheyennes would be found somewhere along the Washita; with a practiced eye Sanjak noted all the signs of human passage, whether of white men, of Cheyennes, or of other tribes. The Wichita uplift, gray and indistinct, rose on his left above the line of timber that bordered the creek; on his right the prairie rolled and dipped until it blended into the leaden-colored sky. A cow appeared on one of the rims, strayed from some cattle drive, and on another a coyote trotted, stopped and stared, and then trotted away, disappearing in one of the draws. With more and more white and unfriendly trespassers upon the plains, and with army patrols on the outlook for straying Indians, Sanjak was more than usually cautious. Once, coming to a rise, he saw a mounted figure in the distance, too far to be distinguished. Instinctively he nudged his pony down into the draw and crept up to where he could peer through the grass. The figure looked like an Indian, but the mount was not a pony; it moved with the gait of the white man's cavalry. The rider might be one of the Osage scouts used by the army. He was motionless, as though surveying the landscape; then presently he set his horse to a canter and disappeared.

After a time Sanjak made his way to where the scout had been, examined the ground, and noticed the shoe marks of an army mount. He followed the trail, keeping well behind, until he saw it join with several others and then with them turn to the northeast.

That night Sanjak camped in a pecan grove in a draw, without lighting a fire, making his supper on jerky and mesquite bread, and sleeping wrapped in his blanket.

The next day he made a long circuit to the north and west, where he found other signs of reconnaissance, and that evening reached the camp of the Cheyennes along the Washita. One of the Cheyennes told him where he might find Black Kettle, some distance down the river.

As he rode down through the lodges set among the timber along the river bottom, Sanjak saw that this was not a war camp. The lodges were not close settled, as for defense, but were scattered for the distance of a half hour's walk the length of the river bottom. The squaws were busy, some dressing skins in the chill air, others cooking stew over twig fires, while children, half-naked and indifferent to the cold, played along the edge of the river, where ice was beginning to form.

Black Kettle welcomed Sanjak with an embrace and led him to his lodge, where he introduced him, by a nod and the mention of a name, to his daughter. She was the squaw of a certain brave who was out looking after his ponies, and with her was her baby, wide-eyed and silent in the papoose carrier.

Black Kettle's squaw, busy over the pot, the chief did not mention. That was understood. Black Kettle settled himself on a buffalo robe, invited Sanjak to his side, and brought out his pipe. When the two had each taken several puffs of tobacco, Sanjak told him of Makin's concern.

The old man meditated for a while, his pipe forgotten in his hand, and presently passed his hand over his head and fingered the thin braids of his gray hair.

"Cheyennes are not on the warpath," he said. "There was trouble in the high plains. Our young men pursuing the buffalo met white hunters. There was a fight. Some white hunters were killed, also some Cheyennes. But it is not cause enough to go on the warpath."

Black Kettle spoke with a composure that could be read as the apathy of age, a weariness from many reverses. Dusk had fallen, and a quiet fell over the great camp. The air grew damp and the chill permeated the lodge.

Sanjak, concerned for the agent's warning, reminded Black Kettle of the massacre of the Cheyennes at Sand Creek in the Colorado territory, when the tribe had camped under army guarantee of protection, with the white man's flag flying from a tall pole. Black Kettle laid aside his pipe.

"Sand Creek will not happen again," he said heavily. "The white men are ashamed. There was much talk about it in the councils of the Great White Father."

"But no punishment of Chivington."

"That may be, but they would not like it to happen again. In any case, I must walk the way of peace. I have said so at the great council of Medicine Lodge, when the tribes all signed the treaty."

The old chief said this with a finality that belied weariness or apathy. His expression was impassive, with the impassivity of tribal authority. Sanjak recognized in him a quality of which he himself partook in part—a set of purpose, a drawing of necessity, as a night-lost wanderer is drawn by a distant fire—and Sanjak was drawn to Black Kettle as a son to a father, eager to learn and to follow.

Still, he remained urgent to impress the agent's warning and his own anxiety. He told Black Kettle of the signs of reconnaissance that he had seen.

"It would be wisdom to change camp," he counseled.

Black Kettle rose and went to the lodge opening. Lifting the flap, he looked out. In the evening light snowflakes were falling, roseate against the somber background of timber.

"This is no weather for the warpath. The white men like to sleep, the same as Indian. Remain the night with us, and tomorrow you will take word to Agent Habercord that Black Kettle is a man of peace, a man of his word, that he does not want trouble with the army."

Sanjak accepted the buffalo robe offered him and drew it over him, but slept lightly. Several times during the night he rose and went out. The snow had continued to fall. It was a wet snow that mantled the trees and formed drifts in the narrow draws that led to the river. As the night grew colder, it formed a crust that crackled in the wind. Yes, this is not a night for the warpath, Sanjak thought.

Shortly before dawn he rose and stepped out again into the open air. The snow had ceased, the sky had cleared, and a yellow moon shed its rays over frozen snow. Some distance away, through the grove of willows a squaw was returning to her lodge, breaking her way through the drifts with faggots for the fire. Suddenly she dropped her bundle and began to scream,

"*Yipari! Yipari!* [Soldiers! Soldiers!]"

Sanjak could see nothing, but in the clear air he could distinguish sounds. From above, on the frozen prairie, came the crunch of snow, the snorting of horses breaking through, and the bark of command. On the instant he was back in the lodge.

"They've come—and it's an attack," he cried as he took up his bow and slipped the quiver strap over his head. Black Kettle donned his ceremonial headdress, an enormous band of eagle feathers embroidered with bead work and brightly painted that fell from head to floor.

"I will go meet them," he said. "We shall deal in peace."

"You will not fight?" Sanjak jerked out the words.

"Nor you. You are a brother, Sanjak, but not a blood brother, or a brother in arms. You are not wearing war paint. Should there be fighting, you will return to your tribe and your people."

"I am your guest, a lodger in your tepee," returned Sanjak. "I will fight at your side."

"But I shall not fight. I have given the white men my word. When Black Kettle is gone, when the Red men are no more, when white men swarm the land as once did the buffalo, they will ask, 'Was there no honor in the Red man?' and they will remember Black Kettle."

"What are you going to do?" shouted Sanjak impatiently.

But there was no opportunity for answer. From beyond and above, at the edge of the draw, where the level prairie dropped toward the river bottom, came the clamor of battle. The troopers had broken into the camp and were firing at the lodges, their fire met by volleys of arrows mingled with occasional rifle and musket shot from those of the Cheyennes who possessed firearms. Along with the sound of fighting, the bark of rifles and whine of arrows, was the commotion of a camp in frenzy of flight. Mingled with the yelling of the troopers and the war shouts of the braves were the screams of squaws, the crying of children, and the snorting of frightened, tethered ponies.

Sanjak's anger, his dismay, his lust for battle, was held by Black Kettle's superior mastery of spirit. He waited with Black Kettle at the lodge opening. The fighting was yet some distance up the river but drawing nearer. The troopers were impeded by the low timber and the brushwood, and the Indians returned fire from clumps and hollows, while the squaws and children ran for the river to seek shelter on the other side.

The troopers now broke through just above, and some with torches were setting fire to the lodges while others galloped along the riverbank firing and slashing with their sabres at every obstacle, whether brave, squaw, child, or tepee.

At his lodge opening Black Kettle stood erect, passive, majestic in his feathered headdress, his arms extended like those of a man signaling semaphore, while he awaited the approach of death. If even he had thought of resistance, it was futile now.

To Sanjak, for a brief moment, he appeared like the image of the man on the cross that hung by a leather thong inside his shirt.

But only for a moment. A charging trooper bore down upon them, firing point-blank as he came. Black Kettle crumpled, and Sanjak caught him as he fell.

The old man died without a word.

For a moment all the conflicting currents of his experience surged together and foamed within Sanjak, the faith he had put in the agent's Christian protestations, Ileeta's insistence upon forgiveness and submission, the fierce tribal resentment of the white man's injustice and cruelty, the primal cry for retaliation—all these rose and beat upon his resolution, his instinct for action, until he had lost all power of will, all power of action.

He continued to hold Black Kettle's still warm but stiffening body in his clasp. Then letting the body slip to the earth, he fitted an arrow.

But it was too late for action. The battle had roared on down the river toward the lodges below. At the river, several of the women, holding babies aloft, were struggling in the current. Sanjak threw his bow away and ran to their assistance.

TEN

"Black Kettle! Where is Black Kettle?" cried Tow-hee, the chief's squaw, in broken Comanche as Sanjak pushed and struggled in the water to get the old woman to the other bank. She kept turning and crying out for her husband.

"Black Kettle has gone to the Sky Father," grunted Sanjak finally. "Come."

The old woman tore herself loose from his grasp and tried to throw herself into the current. "Go!" shouted Sanjak and gave her a push and a slap, and finally reached the bank with her. Behind them was desolation, veiled in a haze of smoke, which deadened also the sound of battle down the river.

"All gone," moaned the old woman over and over, as Sanjak hurried her on through the timber. "No more Cheyenne people. Cheyenne people finished."

It was not quite the case, Sanjak recognized, as later in a bitter mood he brooded at the door of his lodge and considered the condition of his own people. Some of the Cheyennes had survived, but they were only a feeble remnant, poverty-ridden, and now dispersed, their herds driven off, dependent on the government rations for their existence, compelled to till the soil about their hovels for their subsistence.

"Our race is dying," he told himself. "Our livelihood, the buffalo, is being taken from us, and we must eat the white man's meat. For what do we live—to feed on carrion?"

Some of his tribe were trying to follow the white man's road. They had tried to raise cattle, as the white men did, but the cattle strayed, or were stolen by white men, who claimed they had been stolen from the white man's herds, or the cattle died of some murrain or other. The agency had sent to Colorado for sheep—perhaps they would be easier to tend—and a great herd had been driven down from the high plains, but they also all died before they reached the reservation. Some of the tribe planted corn—or made an effort to tend the corn planted for them by Wichitas and Caddoes, who had been accustomed to farming, and who had been hired by the agency to teach their wilder Plains brothers. But jackrabbits nibbled the shoots before they could reach a growth, weeds choked others, and the stalks that reached maturity were wilted by the hot August sun and withered before the ears could form.

And among the few of the tribe who had consented to live in the houses erected for them by the agency, strange illnesses struck. Such things common among the white men as measles, grippe, whooping cough, and diphtheria struck with a savagery worse than any war club, leaving victims dead or maimed or so weakened as to long for death.

The tribe, now taking lesson from the disaster to the Cheyennes on the Washita, no longer kept close-linked, but scattered in their several bands to the limits of the reservation, moving from place to place within their narrowed land like a captured pony pacing in endless circuit of its corral, and returning to the agency only for the sporadic issuance of government treaty goods.

Under the restraining influence of Sanjak, however, the Nut Eater band of Kiowas had kept their movements within a narrower orbit, camping mostly in the lee of the hills and in the timber along the banks of Rainy Mountain Creek. At Sanjak's urging they agreed to receive a visit from the teacher whom Agent Makin had recruited, a soft-voiced and largehearted Quaker known as Thomissey, and under his gentle persuasion and obvious affection, several parents returned their children to this school.

But when one of the Kiowa boys, unhappy at school discipline, fled the schoolroom and returned to the band, Yellow Horse, the valiant leader of the Red Legs, began to agitate for war. He proposed a medicine dance.

"If you listen to the voices of the white man when they sing, you will hear of happenings in the north. The Sioux, the northern Cheyennes, the Ogalalla, all are holding medicine dances. There is a great one among them—a medicine man of much power—who has heard the voice of the white man's messiah. He is saying that the white man's messiah is a messiah for all men—the Red men as well as the white—and that he is coming soon to deliver his Red children.

"Our allies, the Comanches, who have not for many years held the medicine dance, now have determined to hold one. Shall we Kiowas be alone in not holding a dance and invoking the messiah to come and deliver us?"

Some of the Kiowa bands did hold a medicine dance, and the result was that some of their warrior societies went off the reservation on larger raids, taking herds of ponies, and falling into fights with cowmen driving their herds up from Texas to the railhead in the Kansas territory.

These forays went unavenged by the white men, for Agent Makin was firm in his Quaker conviction that he could control his charges with love—aided by no more than a civilian police force he had recruited among the peaceful and agrarian Caddoes. Colonel Grierson protested but continued to accept his edict not to move against the Indians—an effort that would promptly have driven the bands to scatter beyond the limits of the reservation and make the task of their control even more difficult.

Nevertheless, the agent again summoned Sanjak, whom he considered the most amenable among the Kiowas, and upon whom he had come to rely for counsel as well as for intermediation.

"Tell me," he said kindly, after courtesies had been exchanged, "what is this medicine dance of which I hear, and what is its purpose?"

Sanjak struggled with his limited knowledge of English.

"Kiowa people in much trouble. Comanches also in much trouble. They are few, and not many babies born. White people many and many babies born. White men take all our hunting lands, they come and shoot down Cheyennes. At medicine dance we make medicine for many babies, for brave warriors, for help to keep our hunting grounds. Kiowas much hungry."

Agent Makin gave thought to this, walking over to the window of the frame-and-sod house that served as the agency. Before his eyes the prairie stretched yellow and brown to the distant timber of the creek. Returning to Sanjak, he remarked,

"I have heard something of this new messiah talk. In what medicine do you, Sanjak, trust?"

Sanjak was slow in answering as he sought to penetrate the mysteries of both metaphysics and language.

"Many medicines," he said. "Each man has his medicine. Some medicine very powerful. But over all Great Spirit, but what he say nobody know."

Makin mused again before going further, while he laid a stick of locust wood on the hearthfire.

"Spotted Horse Peter is doing well in school. He will go to the dance?"

"Spotted Horse Peter stay here with you."

"Too young?"

"Too young and not too young. If he want to go, he may go, but you tell him to stay here."

"Spotted Horse Peter behaves like a good Christian boy. You like that?"

"I like. His mama Christian. He grow up Christian."

Makin finally came to what he had been wanting to say.

"And you, Sanjak. Do you want to become a Christian?"

"I like, but don't know what is Christian."

"There are many kinds of Christians, as there are many kinds of Indians. But above all one Great Spirit, and one Book that tells us about him. Now, our kind of Christian—the persuasion to which I hold—doesn't believe in talking, at least much. We listen. We listen for the Great Spirit to speak to us. He came among us once in the man Jesus, and to those who believe in Jesus he continues to speak—perhaps not in words, English words, or Kiowa words, but in a voice to be understood. Now, that's all I want of you—just listen, and in proper time the Great Spirit will speak to you loud and clear. Do you understand that?"

Sanjak, for all that troubled him, found his heart momentarily lightened. He recalled again how still water reveals the colored stones in its depths.

"I understand. I have hunted. I fish. I know how to wait on game, how to wait for fish to bite. I can wait for Great Spirit to speak."

He paused and added,

"Does Jesus Spirit answer Indian prayer?"

"He hears every man's prayer, and we are told that he answers the prayer of the faithful. But in his own time, in his own way."

"Will you pray for my people," asked Sanjak humbly, "that Christian Jesus give them good days and many papooses?"

"That I will, Sanjak. But you must pray also. He hears your prayers the same as mine.

"And I want you to do something more. The Great Spirit

154

expects each of us to be his helper. Faith without works is dead, we are taught. I want you to use your influence more than ever to persuade your young braves to peace. I've heard about these affairs. They eat peyote, or something, and work themselves into a frenzy, and then they want to go on the warpath. They'll need the steadying hand of older and wiser men. I want no trouble. You understand? The white man's road is not necessarily the Christian road. I've kept the army away from the Kiowas—troops that have been itching to have a whack at the Red men—but I've so far held them back. When some Comanches had the audacity to steal a string of cavalry mounts right out of the stables, under the very noses of the sentries, you can imagine what the colonel said to me."

Sanjak could not help chuckling at the remembrance. The feat had been well aired throughout the reservation, even it was said among the white men far to the east, with some of them calling for sterner measures against the Indians, and others ridiculing the army for its ineptitude.

"The colonel wanted to lead an expedition forthwith, to redeem his name and to give the Comanches a lesson. But so far I have kept them to their barracks. After all, what are a few dozen horses to the shedding of men's blood? No, we must have peace whatever the cost. And I want you to use your influence to that end."

Sanjak considered.

"Young braves no longer listen to old men," he commented.

"One thing more," added Agent Makin. "The railroad now reaches to Atoka, and freight service begins within a week. This will make the delivery of the rations more regular than has been possible by wagon team. I have ordered a supply of treaty goods to be sent as the first shipment. I beg you, Sanjak, go and give this word to your people."

"I think our people will hold a medicine dance," said Sanjak. "If not, they will be called Caddoes and dogs at the heel of the white men. But maybe, no trouble. We will see."

ELEVEN

For the great medicine dance of the Nut Eater Kiowas there had been erected in an open space in the timber bordering Rainy Mountain Creek a lodge of wythes and brushwood, and covered completely with skins and blankets and army tarpaulins to hide the ceremonial from all but the initiates. It was large enough for fifty men to assemble. An aperture in the roof let out the smoke from the fire that had been burning in the center for several days. The covering of the lodge had been provided by various members of the band, in many cases by stripping their own tepees, for skins were increasingly hard to come by; and building the lodge had been a communal undertaking, in which squaws did much of the heavy work.

The ceremony was also an occasion for testing some of the

novitiates of the society—among whom was Howling Dog, whom Sanjak had been teaching the use of weapons and whom he now thought sufficiently instructed, despite some reservations he had toward the youth. Howling Dog was impetuous, too impetuous, like an overstrung bow that could break when drawn too quickly.

The Red Legs sat around in a circle about the fire, naked save for breechclout, absorbing its heat while the sweat poured from them and dampened the earth on which they sat, washing away the paint with which their bodies were covered. They said nothing, and they did not stir, except that from time to time one might leave the lodge to relieve himself or to admit a young novice with more wood for the fire. From time to time also, as one or another of the young braves seemed about to fall over in stupor or overcome by heat, Yellow Horse, the valiant war chief with the great scar, would revive him by giving him from an army canteen a little water in which various secret herbs had been steeped.

From time to time also, one or another of the young braves would stir from his lethargy and moan or begin an incantation to some secret spirit, and this might go on for some time, when suddenly he would leap to his feet and begin a frenzied twisting of his body, and dance around the fire. In the course of the dance he might slash at his face or his chest or arms with a hunting blade, not enough to injure but enough to draw blood, which flowed at first in fine lines down the body, then a trickle that swelled and mingled with the sweat.

This continued until late into the night, until one or another of the braves fell exhausted and slept. As the morning light crept in, Yellow Horse the indefatigable was awake and arousing the dancers, giving each of them a pellet of pounded venison and a biscuit of baked mesquite meal and another swallow of the medicine water. Gradually the dancing was resumed, but now more lethargically, as weariness gained control, until Yellow Horse entered the circle by the fire and began to harangue the men.

In war talk Yellow Horse was eloquent. He began by re-

157

counting the past glories of the Kiowas, when they rode on the great raids into Mexico and brought back horses and booty and women, and then described their present state of squalor and dependence. He dwelt on the childlessness of the women and the supineness of the men, and then, raising his voice in a sing-song chant, declaimed:

"But now the day has come. I have seen the red star of the evening. And in the night the Great Spirit of the Kiowas appeared to me—in shape like an antlered elk, with a yellow pumpkin caught on the prongs—and spoke to me saying,

" 'People of the Kiowa. You who have kept the calendar stick. The day has come to strike down the white man, to recover your hunting lands, to fill the lodges with red meat, that your women may bear and your young lads grow to become warriors.'

"Let us rise, let us put on the war paint, let us defy the white man and his soldiers and his loud speaking and many talking guns."

There was more, but already the braves, affected by his challenge and the drugged water, were drowning his words in shouts of approval and cries of war.

Sanjak, as an elder member of the Red Legs, had been one of the participants in the dance, but he had refused drink and had remained silent, and for the most part had sat motionless since the dance began.

He was in deep perplexity, as he struggled between the instincts of his race and the traditions of the fathers and the learning he had obtained of the white man and the desire that pursued him over the years to be the person Ileeta had held up to him when she had placed her life in his hands. Now he recalled Agent Makin's injunction to him to pray, and he remembered the English words of the Lord's Prayer that he had been taught.

But in English the words were mostly past his comprehension, and he now tried to put them into the Kiowa tongue.

"O Great Spirit, greater than all the little spirits that inhabit the earth," he prayed. "We listen to your voice, if you shall speak to us. We hearken to your counsel, if we can understand. We stand naked in your presence, as the young initiate of the Red Legs must before the elders if he would enter the society. We ask you to be the father and chief of our people. Tell us when to take up the lodge poles and when to set them down. Lead us, Great Spirit, where the game grazes and the water flows, that we and our children not be hungry. And—"

Here Sanjak's understanding faltered. "Forgive us our trespasses," he did not rightly understand, except, as Agent Makin had taught, it was trespass to steal, to tell a lie, to take another man's wife—but Sanjak had been guilty of none of these. There came to recollection the ancient business with Running Wolf, upon whom he had taken vengeance for what Running Wolf had done to Ileeta. Would the Great Spirit now take such vengeance upon him? He did not know.

Suddenly it came to him as he prayed that should the Great Spirit not take vengeance upon him for his vengeance upon Running Wolf, so should the Kiowas not exact retribution from the white man for all they had suffered at his hands. That, no doubt, was what Agent Makin meant, and what he wanted Sanjak to persuade the band from attempting.

While these thoughts were forming and collecting in Sanjak's mind, ideas of a different sort were taking form and hardening among the Red Legs. They would make a great attack upon the nearest white settlement, slay male and female and carry off all the cattle and children.

It was at this point that Sanjak rose and, by an extended arm, indicated that he had words to speak. When Yellow Horse gave his signal, gradually the young braves quieted.

"Yellow Horse of the great scar is a man mighty in battle," Sanjak began. "His victories are past number. He is protected by powerful medicine that brings him through many battles unhurt. But let me add,

"Do you mount a horse to catch a hare? Do you attack a bear with a sling?"

The young braves in their drugged state gave him curious attention.

"The men of the settlements are not foolish," Sanjak continued. "They also have the fast-speaking guns, in plenty. We are not many, and we can no longer spare the young braves, nor have we tears to weep for those who may not return. There is a better way."

"A better way?" cried out one of the Red Legs.

"The iron road the white men have been building runs now as far as the trader's post at Atoka. Wagons will soon roll upon it, filled with good things for the lodges. Let us be patient, and there will be plenty of meat on the fire, blankets many in the lodges."

Yellow Horse had always been a friend to Sanjak and regarded him as second in command, but now his warrior blood rebelled. He stepped forward and raised his hand.

"Patience!" he exclaimed passionately. "I can have patience pursuing the antelope, whose legs are swifter than mine. But does one need patience to seize a tortoise? One needs only to know how to grasp its neck. Why wait upon the iron road when there are cattle in pens in the ranches and settlements!"

"You think the iron wagons are tortoises?" asked Sanjak, turning and looking at Yellow Horse intently. "You do not know their swiftness. Have you forgotten the wires also that are better than signal fires to carry the news?"

"I have learned about the wires," responded Yellow Horse, "and I know now how to silence them with a blow of my ax. Now let me match my speed against that of the iron wagon. We will attack the wagons and choose for ourselves what we like instead of what the soldiers at Sill give us. But you, Sanjak, shall help us, for you know the iron road from your days in the settlements."

A cry went up in the smoke filled lodge:

"The iron wagons! Scalp the iron wagons!"

The excitement was uncontrollable. Loping Dog, one of the younger braves, with a vast insolence and indifference to danger, began to croon.

"The iron wagons. Sanjak will lead us."

There was a shout of approval.

Upon Sanjak the effect was that of peyote. It had been a long time now since he had been on a raid. Suddenly memories of past adventures, of attack and flight, of pursuit and retreat, rose before him. He saw a Mexican village in flames and the face of a Mexican girl staring in horror as a warrior rushed in and seized her and bore her away. . . .

"I will lead you," he said presently, "but only in my own manner, and all must agree to my command."

Yellow Horse raised his arm.

"Be it so. Sanjak shall lead us."

TWELVE

The moon had set early, and the night was thick from overcast as they rode out toward the east to the edge of the white men's territory. Led by Yellow Horse, whose scent for the trail was like that of the panther for his prey, they came to the Red River. They followed its course downstream for an hour—twenty warriors of the Red Legs—riding in the water where it flowed shallow among the sandbars, and came out through a thick growth of elm and cottonwood and post oak. Here they left the river for a ridge of rock outcropping and then into a prairie of high bluestem grass. In the draw of a creek they camped for the night and at early dawn rode again, across a still uninhabited plain, where the grass was rich but where buffalo no longer roamed.

They rode throughout the fourth day, keeping for cover to the timbered creeks wherever possible, and toward late afternoon they topped a rise and saw below the iron road coursing the valley, following the banks of Elder Creek, twin threads like wire that glistened in the setting sun. Here at Yellow Horse's word they tethered their ponies among the high bushes while they settled down to watch. They took turns watching all night, and the next morning, about two hours after sunrise, one of the watching braves called softly, "There."

Below on the track they saw the fire wagon with big boxes on wheels go by with a great clatter and great clouds of smoke.

They continued to lie in wait, and toward sunset the locomotive and cars returned. When the sun was down, Sanjak signaled for the band to descend to the tracks.

"Now what do we do?" they asked Sanjak, when the young braves saw the size of the rails—as thick as their arms—and how they were held to the crossties by great spikes.

"These wagons are not so good as ponies," explained Sanjak. "They must keep to the rails like horses to a wagon. We will part the rails, and the wagons will tumble over into the ditch."

"Good."

"But we must do so just before the train comes. We will wait and see."

"How so?" one of the warriors, Loping Dog, asked. "To these rails we are like mosquitoes to a sleeping bear. We can only tickle the nose."

Sanjak laughed.

"I have driven many a spike into ties like these, and what I drove in I can draw out."

Sanjak fetched from his sack a short piece of iron he had brought with him that was flattened at the end and forked, like a snake's tongue.

"See," he said, "I thrust this under the head of the spike, and lean so, and out it comes."

The warriors looked on as he went about the task. It was not quite so easy as he had said, but with the aid of some small ballast rocks used for leverage he withdrew one spike, and then another. Presently the task was done.

"Now we wait and see."

They slept through the night, and well before daybreak they ate and tested their weapons. None of them had more than bows and arrows and war axes except Yellow Horse, who had one of the new short guns that could be fired many times, and Sanjak, who had the Spencer he had taken when he left the settlements. At Sanjak's word they found cover among the undergrowth, from where they could rush down and attack as soon as the locomotive was ditched. They waited not long before Loping Dog called,

"Here it comes—but what a little train!"

Sanjak recognized it at once as a road gang's handcar, the kind on which Ole Svenson had ridden into his acquaintance. Two men were on the car, and the car was coming rapidly, for it was going downgrade. As the braves watched, it came on, and as it reached the place where the rails were spread, it struck the ties and bumped along for a moment. Then as the two men jumped off, it leaped and with a lunge went down the embankment.

One of the braves gave a great cry and sent his pony galloping down the slope.

It was Howling Dog, the novice, on his first war party.

"Come back," shouted Sanjak. "They're but workmen."

But Howling Dog was now too excited to be held by words. The two white men had picked themselves up and were clambering up the bank when they caught sight of the Indians, a number of whom had leaped from their cover to follow Howling Dog. With a great effort they managed to set the handcar aright and to put it back on the tracks.

Sanjak noted that one of the two, who had lost his hat, was an older man with little hair on his head.

As the Indians drew nearer, the younger man opened a box on the car and drew out a rifle, and kneeling, took aim and fired.

164

It was Howling Dog, the novice, who took the bullet. He fell on the instant, tumbling from his horse. The others, however, continued to charge. But the men had set the car in motion and it was gathering speed down the slope.

Sanjak looked at Howling Dog, now convulsively twitching in the last agonies of death, and pity mingled with anger rose within him to become fury. In a moment the instincts of war, of blood lust and the urge to destroy, overwhelmed him like a thunderclap and a deluge of rain, washing away all the restraints he had cultivated in his efforts to walk the white man's road. He lifted his Spencer, took aim, and fired. The bullet went true. It struck the older man. He caught at his chest, lurched, and fell from the car.

The car stopped with a squeal of brakes, and the younger man leaped down to rescue his companion. Seizing him by the waist, he lifted him to the car.

But the delay was fatal.

The Red Legs, racing to be the first to count coup, were now upon them. Little Robe, who rode a calico, was first to bring his war ax down. It was upon the head of the younger man, and a terrific blow. The man fell lifeless to the side of the track. Otter Tail finished the other, already wounded and dying, and his body rolled down the bank to the edge of the water.

Sanjak had not joined the rush. The blood lust had left him as rapidly as it had come. He now returned his rifle to its case and prodded his pony down the slope. Little Robe had already taken the scalp of the younger, and Otter Tail that of the elder. He held it aloft by its sparse hair.

"Better a hare now than a buffalo next winter," he cried. In his other hand he held a silver timepiece by its chain, and it had a familiar look to Sanjak as it caught the morning sunlight and threw it into his eyes. "I always wanted a white man's sun piece."

"What do you want the watch for?" asked Sanjak harshly. "One day is the same as another to you."

"It tells me when the sun sets," protested Otter Tail. "I have

165

seen its fingers when it points."

"What are your eyes for?" asked Sanjak sarcastically. "And your nose? A good nose can smell the night coming."

He went over to where the bodies lay.

The old man was lying face up, eyes open and staring toward the buzzards that were already circling overhead.

Sanjak recognized the man. It was Svenson.

Sanjak gazed a long time at the face, still placid in death, as the man had been in life. The braves saw him standing motionless and in his craggy and generally immobile face read an expression that drove them to withdraw and wait. For some little time they kept silence, while overhead the carrion vultures, drawn by the gore below, circled expectantly. In Sanjak the mingled currents of consternation, grief, and remorse struggled for outlet. The men waited, and the sun began to graze the tips of the taller branches of the woods along Elder Creek.

Finally a great shudder rippled over Sanjak's shoulders; he straightened, looked about him, and spoke to the others,

"We will bury them the white man's way."

The young men found this mystifying, but they respected Sanjak for his superior wisdom and experience with the white men and made no question or protest. Among the tools on the handcar were mattock and spade, and with these they set to work, burying the two in adjacent pits by the tracks, and mounding them, and on the top Sanjak laid the tools.

Chastened by the loss of one of their number, the Red Legs lost interest in further assault and, remounting, took the trail back to the tribe.

THIRTEEN

"Sanjak cold? Sanjak sick?" asked Brown Berry, the quiet one, as Sanjak sat day after day in his lodging, not stirring outside, barely tasting the savory stew she set before him.

"Not cold. Not sick."

"You do not eat. You do not like what I cook?"

"What is it?"

"Rabbit."

"Rabbit?"

"No more buffalo meat. Army meat did not come. Last time it was full of worms and I gave it to the dogs. Bird-that-Sings set a trap and caught the rabbit. Rabbit is good. Why don't you eat?"

"I think."

That was an occupation of Sanjak's with which Brown

Berry was well acquainted, and she said no more. Presently however, she tried again, tentatively.

"Warm today. Would Sanjak like to sit in the sun?"

Sanjak rose heavily and moved to the lodge opening, where he sat just outside on a buffalo robe that Brown Berry spread and drew his blanket about him. He sat in the golden sunlight, staring across the prairie, while a sere wind of late autumn blew over him and tossed his braids about his graven and weathered face.

He was thinking, so far as the materials of his experience and the habits of his life permitted, struggling with a great dilemma—but more, struggling to resolve the mood of regret and dissatisfaction with self, of such anguish as he had never before experienced.

Continually there kept rising in memory his days as laborer on the railroad, and the kindnesses Svenson had shown him—the first kindness he had ever received from a white man. It was such kindness, concern, and compassion for a fellow human being as was alien to his tribal culture—a culture that knew rectitude, honesty, honor, courage, indifference to pain, generosity, even a capacity for self-sacrifice for another—but not the persistent goodwill and concern that was a continuing flow like that of the spring that fed Rainy Mountain Creek. Makin had that quality, and other white men he had met—not all, by any means, but enough to know that here lay a difference between the two peoples, not a fundamental difference of structure, heritage, or inborn capacity, but a gift one had received, the other not.

That gift Ileeta had received, and he had tried to possess it in wearing her Medicine, the crucifix she kept on a chain about her neck, and which he now reverently guarded in a leather sack. But for all his listening to the white men who seemed also to possess it, men like Svenson and Makin, it still eluded him. Why had not that power stayed his hand when he raised his rifle and shot his benefactor?

These were questions he asked himself again and again with something akin to remorse. . . .

A jackrabbit—of the kind that simmered in the pot—loped across the prairie in the distance, dun-colored like the prairie, but not so indistinct as to escape Sanjak's lidded gaze. It stopped for a moment, as though itself contemplating the autumn scene, but presently, responding to some inner power, it began loping again. What was that power, Sanjak now asked himself—that thing called life, of which Sanjak had deprived Svenson, whose goodness was like honey found in some forest tree?

It was a question that had never troubled Sanjak. He accepted life as it was, without thinking of it as a gift; he had in his time deprived several others like himself of life without thinking he had separated them from a thing of value. He had put his own life in forfeit with what both white man and Red called courage but was nothing more than indifference to its meaning and worth. It was, indeed, only in these latter years, since Ileeta came into his life, and since his experience in the settlements, that the thought had entered his mind that there was a worth in life itself. It was a thought still inchoate within him, more a feeling, a sense of grasping something not quite like smoke but akin to it. It was a paradox.

Formerly, when he had not a care, or at least when he gave no thought to the morrow, or what or when he should eat, or of provision for the future, when mostly everything pleased him, from the running of rabbits across his trail and the small flowers to the storms and the lightning, liking to lift his face to the rain, in those days he gave no thought to whether the morrow came or not. Now, with a hundred concerns to perplex him, from the rearing of Spotted Horse Peter to the disappearance of the buffalo, the white man's intrusions, the hunger of his tribe, and the delays in the delivery of the rations, the new maladies of the children and the stillbirths of the women, the young men's raids and the threats of reprisal—with all these weighing upon him, he had a continuing hunger for life. Today was not enough; there must be a tomorrow for him to look forward to, in which to finish the thoughts begun today—a tomorrow when present troubles would pass, when the white man's intrusions and the Indians' resentment would cease, a tomorrow when he would again sit in the door of his lodge with Ileeta and watch the sun bathe the prairie in a golden light.

Bird-that-Sings had returned from the creek, where she had been gathering fruit from the persimmon trees and from the other squaws the gossip of the day. It was all about the raid that Limping Pony and Tall Man of the Comanches had led into Texas. They had returned with forty ponies and three scalps.

"Agent Makin is very upset, and colonel is very angry. Colonel says he is sending for the big chief to come and punish the raiders."

"Is there talk of the raid on the fire wagon?" Sanjak asked.

"Of that there was nothing said. It was spoken of, but they say it was the work of the Osage, who know all about fire wagons."

Sanjak grunted in relief.

The Osage, domiciled farther east and more settled and acquainted with the white man, had been ferocious warriors in their time and were regarded still as unpredictable. Their relations with other plains tribes had generally been hostile. Since they in their time had exacted booty and scalps from the Kiowa, it would only be appropriate return to let them bear the accountability for the affair with the track men.

Yes, Sanjak thought, let them answer to the white men.

But even as he so concluded, he became uncomfortable with a new uneasiness. Among his people he would not have hesitated to boast of such an exploit. Why should he hesitate to acknowledge the fact before the white man? It was not fear—at least not fear of reprisal. It was fear of a deeper sort, a fear he could not define but was akin to having displeased someone whose favor he desired, but all the more perplexing since he had long ago become indifferent to any man's favor.

As the evening gathered and a purple dusk spread over the prairie, and here and there the tepees were luminescent from the fires within, Brown Berry timidly urged her lord to return to the warmth of the lodge. Sanjak did not respond but continued to sit and to gaze across the plain and to meditate upon mysteries too great for his comprehension.

Presently he stood and walked out into the tall grass until he stood alone in the midst of the prairie, under the great bowl of heaven, sprinkled like golden dust with myriad stars. He lifted his hands high in appeal, and in a beseeching voice spoke to the night:

"O Great Spirit in the heavens, whose eyes are the stars, whose voice the wind in the grass, whose embrace the air about me, I am but Sanjak, the Kiowa. I would not be the great white chief, or one of the race. I do not ask for their great houses, their mighty fire-breathing engines, their many horses, their much wealth of silver and trinkets and weapons of war. I only ask that you speak to me with the voice of him whom Ileeta loved, whom she called your Son. Let him embrace me as he did her, and pour into me the qualities he gave her, qualities I do not understand, but I too would possess. O Great Spirit, speak to me as you spoke to the fathers, with the voice that my heart hears faintly, like the distant murmur of water in the brook, but cannot read or tell. You speak to the timid whitetail, and he listens, for I see him poised in the grass, ears pricked for the sound of your voice. You speak to the eagle circling above the rocks of the Wichitas, for his circling ceases and he alights upon the pinnacle to listen. Speak to me, O Great Spirit, that I too may hear and understand."

There was no answer from the sky, but the effort had drained Sanjak's spirit as it left his strong body exhausted and weary, and in the emptiness of soul and apathy of body a quieting of all mood and desire settled upon him. He felt himself being surrounded by a kind of peace, like a warming and sleep-inducing air, into which one could settle into dreamless slumber. His mind had not resolved its questions, but its restlessness had passed, and beneath the active mind lay a deeper awareness of answer and release.

He returned to his lodge.

FOURTEEN

The great white chief arrived at Sill a few days later in an army ambulance, accompanied only by an adjutant and a half dozen troopers as escort. At once he summoned the chiefs of the Comanches and Kiowas to appear before him.

The chiefs, offended at this brusque behavior, consulted as to their response.

"Let the great chief visit us," spoke Buzzard Quill of the Kwahadi Comanches, who had come in from the high plains with a band of his braves. "He has traveled this far; let him come the little farther."

The chiefs, much as the idea appealed to them, recognized its futility. But the truculent Buzzard Quill was obdurate.

"For what purpose does he call us?" he asked. "Is it to sit

down and smoke the peace pipe again and drink the white man's firewater? For me, I say let us meet him and face him."

This too was recognized as idle talk for one from whose mouth should issue sage counsel. The meeting would allow the Indians to voice their increasing dissatisfaction with the white man's administration—the delays and insufficiencies in the rations, the white men's poaching on the buffalo grounds, the trespasses of others with their cattle herds. On the other hand, it could be the other way around—the white man's dissatisfaction with the behavior of his Indian wards, and no doubt the raids on the Texas ranches, culminating in the recent foray by Tall Man and Limping Pony and their companions.

After several had given their thoughts, the aging Cow-with-a-Hump, the sage of the Kiowas, gave his counsel.

"This white chief sent among us is a noted warrior, but like many warriors is feeble in counsel. It is said that when he sees a hill he knows not to go around but only to climb over. So I have heard as he drove his fellow men into the sea. But he is also, I have heard, a man of law, who does justice by his book. Let us keep our patience and try his. Let us keep silent and let him question as he will, but discover for himself. It is the white man's law that he must have witnesses before condemning. Let us therefore keep silence."

The counsel was good, and it was agreed that old Cow-with-a-Hump should speak for all or keep silence for all. The chiefs proceeded to the post, trailed by a pride of young braves, who were looking for excitement and hoped for a showdown with the white men.

The great war chief of the white men was sitting in a rocking chair on the gallery of the long house, his feet resting on the railing while he smoked a long yellow-brown cigar. He took his feet down from the railing as the chiefs appeared, but continued to smoke his cigar and did not rise and greet the chiefs as they stood wrapped in blankets and dignity, wearing their ceremonial headdresses. The gallery was empty save for the general, his adjutant, and a sentry at each end.

THE KIOWA

Sanjak noticed that the windows along the gallery, generally open to show their glass panes, were now closely shuttered. The house faced a stone-walled corral, behind which the army mounts were kept. Old Cow-with-a-Hump, bent in his limbs, now sat down in the grass before the house, and the other chiefs followed his lead, while the young braves and a number of children and squaws who had followed the chiefs gathered in a wide semicircle in the corral.

The great chief was a slight man; his face was half-hidden by his wide-brimmed hat, all dusty and gray; his blue eyes were narrow and red-rimmed from dust, and his scraggy beard needed combing. His uniform was dusty and stained, and his boots were unpolished.

Presently he crushed out his cigar, cut off the burnt tip with a pocket knife, and after putting the stub in his pocket began to speak.

"I have long heard of the people known as the Lords of the South Plains, the Comanches, and their warlike allies the Kiowas. You are feared by the Apaches, the Pawnees, the Osages, the Wichitas, and others I may mention. I have heard also that you are the finest horsemen on the plains, rivaled only by the Cheyennes."

He spoke evenly, calmly, and waited for the interpreter. A Caddo by the name of Johnny Corncake translated into Comanche. The chiefs nodded in silence.

"I have also heard that there are none braver nor more fierce in battle than the Kiowas."

The chiefs nodded again but said nothing.

"But I find," continued the great war chief, speaking now with more edge, but still calmly, if somewhat more firmly, "that you are a race of cowards and liars."

He waited for this to be translated, but if it had any effect it was not discernible. The Indians remained stoically silent.

"While your white brothers were having difficulties among themselves and had to withdraw their forces from the frontier, your so-called braves, breaking the treaties they had made, marauded into Texas and beyond, burning ranches, slaying the men, and carrying off women and children and herds.

"When our war was ended, we again came among you and negotiated with you. The treaty at Medicine Lodge, by which we assigned you broad and ample lands in which to roam and hunt the buffalo, was made only on condition that you not molest the white settlers beyond the rivers that marked your preserves."

The great war chief rose and paced leisurely along the gallery, revealing for the first time any shade of feeling. But he again took his chair and, after rocking back and forth for a minute, continued,

"Nay, but the Great White Father has done more. He has sent among you good men, men of God, to show you the way of peace, to provide for your necessities, to see your children schooled and educated, to lead you from the darkness of superstition into the way of light and innocence.

"But how have you received these marks of kindness? How have you responded to the wand of gentleness? You have taken kindness for weakness, and gentleness you have counted as dung to be despised. You have, in short, taken our forbearance as fear, and your liberty as license, and have gone rampaging and marauding and dealing death and destruction upon your friends. We have counted forty lives you have taken, one way or another, in the past year."

Again, as this was translated, the lidded and red-rimmed blue eyes surveyed the Indians before him, but if they were inwardly moved by these allegations they did not show it.

"And now," he resumed in a firmer but still even voice, "there has come to me the news of these latest outrages, one upon a company of peaceful teamsters in which three were killed, slain for no more than a string of ponies."

Cow-with-a-Hump rose painfully to respond, but Buzzard Quill stood up first and gathered his blanket about him as sign that he would speak. Cow-with-a-Hump courteously gave way and resumed his place, but there was an audible rustle among the crowd of Indians behind the fence.

"The great war chief honors his Indian brothers by this visit," Buzzard Quill began, ignoring the charges. "We are glad he has come to see how we fare. We welcome him to our lodges, where he may see our children, and feel the bones of their ribs, and dip his spoon into our pots and take up the salt water that serves us as soup, for that the beeves and the flour and the sugar and the coffee that were promised us in exchange for the broad prairies we yielded to the white men are provided us but rarely and insufficiently to stop the cries of hunger that rise in the lodges.

"We welcome the great war chief, and we trust he will accompany us to the Washita, where lie the bones of one hundred twenty Cheyenne braves, squaws, and children. We will show him the ashes of fifty-five lodges that once were covered by over a thousand buffalo robes, and show him also the skeletons of over seven hundred ponies slain by the white man's soldiers.

"What else would our distinguished guest behold? Perhaps you will travel across our prairies and see the bleaching bones of buffaloes without number, slain by hired buffalo hunters, that there be grass for the white man's cattle and land for the white man's plow. Or would you see the graves of our children, stricken down by the white man's ailments hitherto unknown among us? And when you have seen these things, will you not return and tell the Great White Father that we Comanches and Kiowas have seen the white man's road, and have put our feet upon it, but we no longer like it; we prefer the road our forefathers trod."

All this had been said in great dignity, slowly, with kingly gestures and solemn silences as the words were translated. It was evident that the Caddo had poorer command of English than of Comanche, and that much that Buzzard Quill said had not penetrated to the white war chief. When the Caddo had finished, the great white chief rose from his rocking chair and again took a turn up and down the gallery. Then pausing and facing the chiefs before him, he said,

"We must have peace on these prairies. Before the white

"We must have peace on these prairies. Before the white man came, the Indians warred among themselves—Kiowas and Comanches against the Osages and the Pawnees, the Cheyennes against the Utes and the Apaches, and all against the Tonkawas and the Wichitas, for that they were peaceful.

"We have come to bring peace and order and justice, and when you accept these things then will your lodges be full of meat, and your camps again swarm with children, your wives no longer barren, and no longer widows. Now you have broken the law we have given you. You have left the reservations assigned to you, and in the white man's territory you have recently taken three lives and many ponies besides. As chiefs you must bear responsibility. Therefore I demand that you deliver to me the leaders of this raid against the teamsters, that they may be sent to Fort Richardson to be tried for murder before a judge."

There was silence at this before Buzzard Quill again spoke.

"If the man is a judge, then his justice is for the white man and the Red man alike. You accuse us of the lives of three white men. Are the lives of these white men to be weighed against one hundred twenty Red men?"

The white general understood the reference to the Washita massacre.

"That was a mistake—a grievous mistake," he said.

"Has Yellow Hair been punished?" asked Buzzard Quill.

"We are talking now about the murder of three Texas teamsters," said the great chief shortly, "and I don't intend to be drawn aside. Which of you led the raid into Texas?"

But Buzzard Quill was not daunted.

"Does not the white man have a saying, 'You must catch your rabbit before you eat it'? You know where your white chief Yellow Hair is. Should you not judge him before you pursue the other?"

The general cursed and stamped his foot.

"Don't play with me," he exclaimed violently. "Who is the murderer?"

At this Buzzard Quill kept silence.

"No answer? Then you are all guilty. I charge you all with murder and will have you all in Richardson. Surrender!"

This was the expected moment. Buzzard Quill threw back his blanket, and in his hand was a revolver. Limping Pony, sitting on the ground, did the same, revealing a Spencer rifle. Others had bow and arrows. A cry arose among the young braves and squaws who had gathered in the corral and spread across the prairie, reaching the agency, where the distribution of rations was going on, and from all directions Indians came galloping on horse or running to the defense of their chiefs.

"We do not leave the reservation," announced Buzzard Quill.

The white war chief raised his hand. The shutters along the gallery flew open, disclosing at each window a kneeling trooper, rifle cocked and pointed. A bugle sounded, followed by a shout of command, a clatter of hoofs, and the squealing of horses, as from around the ends of the barracks a troop of cavalry galloped up with sabres drawn and surrounded the Indians.

Buzzard Quill shouted,

"We do not go. We die here," and raised his pistol.

At that moment Sanjak lunged forward and knocked the weapon from the chief's hand.

"I go, I go," he shouted in English. "I go to Richardson." To the chiefs, "Put down. Put down. Let them kill me, but not our people."

Sanjak's cry, the presence of the troopers, the logic of the situation were all compelling.

For his part the white general saw also the inadvisability of arresting all the chiefs. He did not want war. He signaled, and one of the sentries hurried down and put manacles on Sanjak.

After a while, when the turmoil had abated, the white chief studied Sanjak, standing before him. He asked his name.

"Sanjak?" He mused as he turned to his adjutant and spoke in a whisper, then returned to Sanjak. "Sanjak," he repeated. "I believe there is a warrant outstanding in Kansas for your arrest for murder and for jumping parole. You will now return to stand trial, and this will let our Red brothers know that the arm of the Great White Father is long, and his justice relentless."

He turned to the chiefs.

"Go!" he commanded. "We release you. This man we will keep as hostage. Return to your lodges."

FIFTEEN

The provost of the day allowed Sanjak to send for Spotted Horse Peter to come to him in the jail cell of the post—an earthen-floored and adobe-walled room with a narrow iron-barred window that looked out on the Wichitas. It was early in the morning, and a crepuscular light filled the cell. Sanjak, as his son entered, was sitting on his heels wrapped in a blanket, his eyes fixed on the rocky heights of the uplift where he had laid Ileeta to rest. The boy waited for his father to speak. Presently, as the light gathered, Sanjak turned and using English, addressed his son.

"What you think of white man?"

"I think very much."

"I know," said Sanjak. "Much. But which way you think—up, down, sideways?"

Spotted Horse Peter wrinkled his nose. In the colder light of day he could see his father's features now clearly—on his forehead and in his cheeks the lines of age and experience, his braids thinner with streaks of gray, his eyes dark and unblinking.

"Some good, some bad, some like falling maple leaves, turn over and over."

Sanjak was silent. He wanted to talk about life and death, upon which he had meditated much of late, and he sensed that in the fresh, untroubled mind of his son he might find wisdom and insights into his dilemma. But he did not know how to broach the subject. Instead, he asked him again what he was learning in school.

Spotted Horse Peter told him about the games he was learning to play. He spoke of a certain game in which the player was called dead.

"That game no good," commented Sanjak. "Not good to kill."

His son laughed.

"No kill. Just for the game. Then come back to life."

"What you know about dying and coming back to life?"

"Teacher say we all die, and at end everybody raised to life, when good will be gathered together and bad sent away."

"Sent away? Where to?"

But this was beyond Spotted Horse Peter. Some things were not clear.

"Who are the bad?" persisted Sanjak.

"Those who do not love Great Spirit and his works." That much he seemed to know.

Sanjak spread his arms exultantly.

"I love everybody. Then I go with the good."

But even as he said this, he was aware that it was more hope than a fact, a sense of benevolence and goodwill toward which he strained but did not possess. A burden of dissatisfaction still pressed upon him. It was an awareness that his deeds did not measure up to that standard of behavior. Why this strange questioning of his own behavior—an attitude of self-examination alien to his culture? It had to do with what Svenson had called a sense of sinfulness. It had to do, he realized, with what these others who called themselves Christians had told him about the god they worshiped, and his demands upon those who worshiped him—the god Ileeta had worshiped and whose goodness Sanjak had persistently sought to comprehend.

Along with this was a paradox that mystified him the more. The more one entered into the life and demands of the god, and the closer one drew near to him, the more aware one became of separation from him by reason of what was now sin that before was not. At the same time, as the sense of separation increased, so did the sense of nearness. Those who freely talked of this unworthiness seemed most filled with a contentment and well-being and benevolence, so that they could say in truth, "I love everybody."

That was the mystery Sanjak now sought to unravel in his distress. He yearned to stand in that light, to feel that enveloping love of and for the god, which he had found in those others, that was like a cooling breeze in summer and a warming fire in winter. If not for himself, then for his son.

"You now read well the white man's books?" he asked Spotted Horse Peter.

"I can read some."

"What book you like best?"

"The God book."

"Many tales in that book. I have heard them. Which you like best?"

"About David."

"*Ai, ai.* You are still a boy and would take scalps. That not good. What about the man who died on the cross?"

"I cry. Very sad."

"Do you say prayers to the man god?"

"I think so."

"I mean, does he hear you?"

"Yes."

"I am going away. Not come back. You pray for me?"

"Yes. But where you go?"
Sanjak lifted his hands by way of reply.
"You'll remember me?"
"Yes. Oh, yes."
"You say prayers for me?"
"Yes."
"You Christian. You not forget."
"Not forget."
"Not forget?"
"Not forget."
"You look after Brown Berry and Bird-that-Sings—take good care of them, not let them be sad—you teach them what you have learned so maybe they become Christian too?"
"I do."
"Good. Now you go."

Early in the morning, while hoarfrost lay on the prairie like a myriad of pearls, Sanjak was taken from the jail house to the headquarters for the preparation of the documents for the court. He had slept well. His interview with his son had left him with a contentment that was like sweet honey after the doubtings and perplexities and anguish of the day before. He thought Spotted Horse Peter was well on the Christian way, and that would be pleasing to Ileeta. As for himself, he was past caring. Whatever he had done or not done he would lay in the man god's lap and let him decide. For an Indian, he had done well. He had cared for his son and his squaws, he had given the tribe good counsel, he had shown the young men bravery in battle, generosity in victory, patience in defeat. He had tried.

At the provost's office a sergeant handed Sanjak some dungarees and ordered him to put them on in place of his Indian dress. As Sanjak did so, the sergeant noticed the leather sack hanging from a rawhide thong about Sanjak's neck.

"Let's see that," he commanded, and Sanjak gave it to him. The sergeant opened the sack and drew out Ileeta's crucifix. After studying it a moment, and turning it over in his palms, he asked in a tone of curiosity,

"Are you a Catholic?"

"What's a Catholic?"

"That crucifix—aren't you a Christian?"

"No Christian, but this is my god."

The sergeant studied the crucifix anew.

"Mexican," he commented. "Loot from one of your raids, eh. Well, Charley, since you're not a Christian, you won't need it."

With a bowie knife he slashed the sack and pocketed the crucifix.

"No, no!" cried Sanjak in sudden consternation. "No steal. Mine. My god. Give it me."

The guards seized Sanjak and held him as he struggled. The sergeant regarded him with an impersonal sympathy.

"Calm yourself, Charley. If it's yours, you will get it back— if you don't hang. It'll be in safekeeping."

"But, before God," he added with sudden vehemence, "no infidel is going to use a crucifix for a totem and good luck if I can help it. I'm a Catholic myself, and I don't go for blasphemy."

Sanjak's contentment disappeared. Mechanically he allowed himself to be led manacled to an open wagon in which were some sacks of grain and some hay, and he was directed to get in. The morning was cold. A blanket was tossed to him, and he wrapped himself in it, covering his head in it. In the wagon with him was an overcoated infantryman with a rifle, who sat huddled against the grain sacks with the brim of his hat pulled down against the brilliant morning sun. Accompanying the wagon was a lieutenant of cavalry and six cavalrymen. Ahead were six other wagons returning to Richardson for army supplies. The lieutenant was apparently new to the plains, for he kept his mount curvetting about the wagon while he scanned the horizon in all directions as if expecting an attack from a horde of Indians.

Sanjak drew his blanket closer over his head, and began to croon a tune Svenson used to sing in his particular English and of which Sanjak had remembered fragments.

Now the day is over,
Night is drawing nigh. . . .

The lieutenant, pausing a moment in his rounds, listened and was puzzled, but then began his restless patrol.

Another heard his crooning, a Caddo, as the escort halted at the advance patrol station. He called to the lieutenant.

"Chief in wagon—he sing death chant—better watch him."

Sanjak was indeed now singing his tribal chant to the tune of the evening hymn.

O sun, O stars and sky—
You abide forever,
But we earthborn must die.

Like the drifting clouds are we
We cast our shadow upon hills and plains
Then travel on—to where, O where?

As he sang of clouds and of rainfall, there returned to Sanjak's remembrance certain things Agent Makin had said about the man Jesus:

"He is like water," said the agent, "that cools the thirst, and cleanses the body, and refreshes the field to cause the grass to grow. Water always seeks the lowest ground, and does not, like the destroying fire, seek to ascend to heaven. So does he, our Lord, abase himself. And so must we, like the water, humble ourselves and seek not our will but his. We must, like water, be content to sink ever lower and lower in humility and obedience, until we reach the Great Water, which receives our eternal spirit into its bosom."

While Sanjak continued to chant his death song, shrouded by his blanket, in the knowledge that the white man's prison would be like the grave, or worse, he tried to fathom the agent's remembered words.

He must submit himself; that was their meaning. He must go down into the white man's prison uncomplaining and

185

silent. There he would be held still and silent as water confined, and there he might see into the depths of his heart and discover the meaning of his life. Perhaps there he would find the union with the Great Spirit. Perhaps there he would find the answer to the perplexities of the Christian way.

And at that moment there returned to recollection the hymn that had been sung at Svenson's church, when he gave the invitation to come forward and receive the Lord Jesus, words sung again and again until they had lodged in Sanjak's memory waiting, it seemed, for the God-given moment to return and answer his deepest longing:

> Just as I am, without one plea,
> But that thy blood was shed for me,
> And that thou bid'st me come to thee,
> O Lamb of God, I come! I come!

And with a sudden easing of his disquiet, and a new sense of contentment, he experienced a release of the spirit that could not be contained. With a cry of triumph and joy he leaped to his feet and began to shout in English.

"I come. I come."

The startled guard sprang after his ward and grappled him. But Sanjak, with a powerful thrust, threw him off and jumped from the wagon. With his manacled hands held high above his head, he began to run across the prairie toward the west, away from the sun, toward the high plains where buffalo still roamed, shouting in English as he ran,

"I come. I come."

It was an action at once premeditated and unpremeditated, at once a flight from reality and a return to reality, an action both of fear and of confidence, a rush both of despair and of joy toward a vision both personal and divine, a response to an experienced personal love and a primal remembrance of a divine love—the final effort of an untutored and unlettered savage to find perhaps in self-annihilation the mystery of his being if not that of existence itself.

186

"Come back!" bawled the lieutenant, reining up and momentarily stupefied, unable to think of more to do than command, "Come back!"

Not far away the level prairie was broken by a deep gully, the effect of winter erosion that lay bare the red earth in a miniature canyon. Sanjak was almost to the gully, still shouting with his manacled hands above his head, "I come. I come."

The lieutenant now roused himself.

"Don't let him reach the gully," he yelled, and then frantically, "Shoot him," and uncontrollably, "Kill him. Kill him."

The troopers, taking the command, raised their rifles and fired. Sanjak stumbled, but gathered his strength and staggered on. Another volley, and he was mortally hit, and fell sprawling.

One of the troopers galloped to where the Indian lay.

"He's dead, sir."

The lieutenant, unable to comprehend what he had done, sat on his mount for some minutes, recovering his composure. He would have to make a report, of course. He wasn't quite sure how it would be received. The prisoner was trying to escape, there was no doubt of that, but to assure himself, he raised the question.

"The prisoner was trying to escape, you saw that?"

The sergeant nodded.

"Yes, sir."

"He refused to halt at command."

"Yes, sir."

"Well," he consoled himself uneasily, "we've saved the government the expense of a trial. Fetch the body."